Praise for th

"Daley's characters come to life on the page. Her novels are filled with a little mystery and a little romance which makes for a murderous adventure."

– Tonya Kappes,
USA Today Bestselling Author of *Fixin' To Die*

"Daley's mysteries offer as much sizzle and pop as fireworks on a hot summer's day."

– Mary Kennedy,
Author of The Dream Club Mysteries

"I'm a huge fan of Kathi's books. I think I've read every one. Without a doubt, she's a gifted cozy mystery author and I eagerly await each new release!"

– Dianne Harman,
Author of the High Desert Cozy Mysteries

"Intriguing, likeable characters, keep-you-guessing mysteries, and settings that literally transport you to Paradise...Daley's stories draw you in and keep you glued until the very last page."

– Tracy Weber,
Agatha-Nominated Author of the Downward Dog Mysteries

"Daley really knows how to write a top-notch cozy."

– *MJB Reviewers*

"Kathi Daley writes a story with a puzzling cold-case mystery while highlighting...the love of home, family, and good friends."

– *Chatting About Cozies*

Snowmen
IN
PARADISE

**The Tj Jensen Mystery Series
by Kathi Daley**

Snowmen

A
TJ JENSEN
MYSTERY

IN

PARADISE

KATHI DALEY

HENERY PRESS

SNOWMEN IN PARADISE
A Tj Jensen Mystery
Part of the Henery Press Mystery Collection

Second Edition | September 2016

Henery Press, LLC
www.henerypress.com

Trade Paperback ISBN-13: 978-1-63511-093-7
Digital epub ISBN-13: 978-1-63511-094-4
Kindle ISBN-13: 978-1-63511-095-1
Hardcover ISBN-13: 978-1-63511-096-8

Printed in the United States of America

This book is dedicated to my super-husband Ken for allowing me time to write by taking care of everything else.

ACKNOWLEDGMENTS

They say it takes a village and I have a great one.

I want to thank all my friends who hang out over at my Kathi Daley Books Group page on Facebook. This exceptional group help me not only with promotion but with helpful suggestions and feedback as well.

I want to thank the bloggers who have pretty much adopted me and have helped me to build a fantastic social media presence. There are too many to list but I want to specifically recognize Linda Langford for her encouragement and friendship.

I want to thank my fellow authors who I run to all the time when I don't know how to do something or how to deal with a situation. I have to say that the cozy mystery family is about as close-knit a family as you are likely to find anywhere.

I want to thank Bruce Curran for generously helping me with all my techy questions and Ricky Turner for help with my webpage.

I want to thank my graphic designer Jessica Fisher for all my flashy ads and headers.

I want to thank Randy Ladenheim-Gil for making what I write legible.

I want to thank Art Molinares for welcoming me so enthusiastically to the Henery Press family and a special thank you to Erin George and the entire editing crew who have been so incredibly awesome and fun to work with.

And last but certainly not least, I want to thank my super-husband Ken for allowing me time to write by taking care of everything else (and I mean everything).

CHAPTER 1

Monday, February 10

"Okay, can I have everyone's attention?" Tj Jensen, Serenity High School's favorite teacher, coach, and choir director, shouted over the drone of the multiple conversations echoing throughout the room. The biggest storm of the year was barreling down on the alpine hamlet of Serenity, Nevada, causing a hyperactive frenzy that threatened to give her migraine a migraine. Not that the snow wasn't timely. The annual winter carnival was scheduled to begin in ten days, and the four feet of powder the National Weather Service had predicted to fall over the next forty-eight hours would be a welcome event.

"We have a little over a week until the concert and we're nowhere close to being ready," Tj continued as the drone settled to a hum. "I plan to devote every class period between now and then to rehearsal, but if we're going to put on the spectacular show I know you would all like to deliver, we're going to need extra sessions after school."

"What about the downhill team?" Blond-haired blue-eyed school heartthrob Connor Harrington had recently been voted captain of the snowboard team and seemed to be taking his new responsibilities seriously. "I thought you were planning to spend every day after school on the mountain with us. The team needs a good showing if we're going to make nationals. I get the fact that this choir thing is important to the school, but with regionals coming up, the downhill team needs to practice every day."

Tj smiled as she tucked a lock of hair behind her ear. Connor had just presented the perfect segue to the news she needed to share with the misfit band of students that made up the newly established Serenity High School Choir. When she'd first been assigned the task of making the group into a *real* choir, capable of competing in regional competitions, she'd truly believed the task impossible. But now? Somehow the mismatched group had bonded to form a show choir worthy of competing for a title. The group's first official performance was scheduled for the opening ceremonies of the winter carnival, which would provide a good dress rehearsal for the official competition season, beginning in March and concluding in May. Tj really wanted her ragtag choir to make a good showing, but first she needed to coach her downhill team to a regional title, starting with the competition against their arch-rival, Beaver Creek, during carnival week.

"I agree that working with the downhill team has to be my priority during the peak of the race season," Tj answered. "Beginning today, I've arranged for the team to have two hours on the mountain every afternoon and all day on Saturday. Obviously I can't be in two places at one time, which is why I asked my good friend, Kyle Donovan, to help out with the choir. Before he moved to Serenity three months ago, he was the lead singer of his own band, and he has an extensive background in both modern and classical music. He's a super-nice guy with awesome ideas and he should be here right about," Tj paused as Kyle entered the classroom, "now."

The kids were going to love him. At least the girls would. Not only did he have the musical background Tj lacked, but with his wavy blond hair, deep blue eyes, and exceptional physique, he was drop-dead gorgeous as well. As lead singer of his own rock-and-roll band, he projected an image Tj was certain the fourteen members of her choir would respond to. Tj watched as Kyle stopped to speak to several of the students who were bombarding him with questions as he made his way to the front of the room. She'd first met Kyle while he was in town for a job interview the previous October. As can happen when big moments collide with unforeseen destiny, Tj and Kyle had forged a special bond in the face of tragic events, and in the short time he'd lived in her small hometown, he'd become one of Tj's most trusted friends.

"My plan," Tj continued, as Kyle managed to separate from the pack and make his way forward, "is to work on the group numbers during our fifth-period class and then have Kyle work with each of the small groups after school. Since the three members of the choir who are also members of the ski and snowboard team haven't been assigned to small groups, there shouldn't be a conflict."

"Coach Jensen," Marley Davis, her least talented yet most vocal student, raised her hand. "As the natural leader of the choir, I think I should work closely with Kyle, sort of as an assistant."

Tj rolled her eyes as Marley tossed her thick black hair over one shoulder and smiled coyly at the man, who was almost old enough to be her father. Marley was smart, rich, and annoying as hell. There was no way Tj was going to saddle Kyle with Marley's irritating presence for any longer than was necessary.

"I appreciate the offer, but I think Kyle will be fine on his own."

"But Coach Jensen," Marley whined as her green eyes narrowed and her full lower lip protruded in a well-rehearsed pout, "I think you're failing to consider that..."

Tj closed her eyes and counted to ten as Marley made her case. She prided herself on getting along with almost anyone, but Marley had been stretching her last nerve since the first day of class. Not only was the establishment of a choir, and Tj's subsequent assignment as its reluctant director, Marley's idea in the first place, but as student body president, she assumed she would be handed a leadership role in spite of the fact that she couldn't carry a tune in a bucket. When Tj refused to be pressured into doing things her way, she'd refocused her energy from bossing everyone around to driving everyone crazy with incessant nagging and tooth-grating complaining.

"You know, Coach," Kyle winked to let Tj know he understood what he was getting into, "I really could use an assistant. Someone to run errands and operate the recording equipment; that type of thing."

Tj shrugged. "Okay, it's your show." The *it's your funeral* was implied. "Marley, you can assist Kyle, but only until the concert."

"Thanks, Coach Jensen."

As the final bell rang, Tj gathered the pile of books and file folders on her desk and entered the crowded hallway, where kids of all ages were running for the exits. She headed toward the administration building, which was centrally located to serve both the elementary and the high school. Serenity High School and Serenity Elementary School had been built on the same plot of land, with a common library, administration office, and cafeteria. The town didn't have a middle school per se. The elementary school housed grades K-7, while the high school handled grades 8-12. Large beige buildings with multiple wings and indoor walkways had been laid out in a pattern Tj likened to a giant spider caught in a web. The situation was ideal for Tj, since she was able to drive her two half-sisters to school and then walk through the covered halls from the elementary school to the high school, where she taught classes every day.

"Brittany," Tj shouted at the tall blond-haired senior over the thunder of lockers slamming in the background.

"Hey, Coach, what's up?" The co-captain of the downhill team, Brittany Baxter, jogged over to where Tj was maneuvering the obstacle course created by bodies in motion.

"I need to stop off to speak with Principal Remington before I head up to the mountain. Can you let the team know that I might be a few minutes late, but I'll be there?"

"Yeah, no problem. Everyone is stoked about all the new powder." Brittany's blue eyes sparkled with enthusiasm as they veered into the school library, where Tj dropped a pile of books into the return bin. "Connor and a couple of the guys cut sixth period and headed over to the mountain early."

"I know everyone is excited, but I really wish they hadn't done that." Tj sighed as they crossed the hall to the front office, where she checked her messages and turned in her attendance paperwork. "I get the allure of fresh snow, but, as ridiculous as this may sound, there are actually teachers who think classes like math and science are equally as important as demolishing Beaver Creek in the downhill competition next week."

Brittany laughed. "That's why you're so awesome. Even though you don't support the guys cutting sixth period and feel compelled as a teacher to show your disapproval, deep down you understand why they might and are therefore disinclined to narc them out."

"Am I that transparent?"

"Totally."

"You know I should contact their parents or assign detention at the very least. It is, after all, school policy. We can't have students cutting class whenever the mood strikes."

Brittany smiled. "Don't worry. I think today's absenteeism was a one-time thing brought on by powder fever. I'm sure everyone will be in class tomorrow."

"Let's hope so. I'd rather like to keep my job." Tj sorted through the paperwork in her box, tossing out a reminder to sign up for direct deposit. One of the toughest things Tj had to learn when she made the transition from student to teacher was that it was her job to make sure the rules were followed whether she agreed with them or not. Tj the student would have cut class in a minute if there was fresh powder to be had, but Tj the teacher was responsible for discouraging such behavior among her students. The only negative comment on her last employee review had been that her students tended to look at her as a friend rather than an authority figure. "I should be able to get to the mountain by three thirty. We'll meet at the base of Grizzly Run. I figure we might as well start with both men's and women's slalom. If you could pass the word along not to be late, that would be awesome."

"Don't worry, Coach," the tall blonde repeated. "I'll get everyone rounded up."

Tj watched Brittany jog away. The poor girl had had a rough year with the breakup of her parent's marriage, but in spite of the turmoil at home, she continued to be Tj's most reliable student. Tj was going to miss her when she graduated in the spring. One of the hazards of being a teacher was that every spring you said goodbye to the seniors you'd grown to love during the four years you'd coached and mentored them. A few of the students chose to stay on in Serenity rather than going to college, a handful more came back afterward, but the vast majority were never heard from again.

Tj waved to Leslie Grayson, her sister Ashley's third-grade teacher. Ashley had begun the year on a rocky note, but things seemed to have calmed down as the sensitive little girl had finally accepted the death of her mother and the subsequent changes to her life. Still, Tj tried to keep an open dialogue with Leslie in the hope of avoiding trouble in the future.

"I'm glad I ran into you." Leslie smiled as she approached Tj. "I was going to call you later this afternoon."

"What's wrong now?" Tj asked. Calls from Leslie were never good news.

"Ashley got into a fight with Loretta Baldwin during second recess."

Tj felt her heart sink. "I thought she was doing better." The first couple of months of school, Ashley had gotten into a number of fights with the students in her class, but after what had seemed to be a breakthrough the previous October, things had gotten much better.

"She was," Leslie confirmed. "She's been happy and agreeable and making friends. I have to admit I was as shocked as anyone when Loretta told me Ashley had ambushed her while she was waiting in line for the monkey bars."

"Do you know what caused the fight?"

"Neither girl is talking, but I have a hunch it has something to do with Loretta's birthday party."

"Birthday party?" Tj asked. "Ashley hasn't mentioned anything about a birthday party."

"That's because she wasn't invited," Leslie admitted. "To make matters worse, Loretta invited the entire class with the exception of Ashley. It's going to be a big event, with a bounce house, a magic show, and an ice-cream bar."

Tj wanted to say that she didn't blame Ashley for punching Loretta, but for once she held her tongue. Siding with Ashley when she acted out had hurt rather than helped the girl's case in the past. "Do we know why Ashley was excluded?"

Leslie began sorting through the mail in her own staff mailbox. "I suspect it has to do with the incident during the field trip to the zoo."

Tj knew that Ashley had pushed Loretta into a pile of camel droppings after Loretta made a comment about the fact that Ashley's mother had died because she was an irresponsible drunk. Tj didn't condone what her half-sister had done, and their mother *was* an irresponsible drunk who had lived a life filled with bad choices that eventually led to her death, but to rub it into Ashley's face was uncalled for. Tj suspected that Loretta's stuck-up snob of a mother had filled Loretta's head with this information in the first place. Serenity was a small town, and although her mother hadn't spent any significant amount of time in the area for over twenty years, her deficiencies as a mother still tended to be part of the local gossip playlist.

Tj sighed. "I'll talk to her. Will there be other consequences?"

"I talked to Loretta's mother. She wants Ashley to be suspended but has agreed to settle for an apology because Loretta wasn't really hurt. Ashley has been given detention and will need to remain inside the classroom with me during recess for the time being. Did you ever look into that counseling we talked about?"

"No," Tj admitted. "Ashley seemed to be doing so much better. I'll look into it."

"I think that would be best."

Tj felt like crying as she continued down the hall for her

meeting with the principal. The last thing she needed was for the behavior of one mean little girl to unravel everything she had worked for over the past several months. The previous July, Ashley's world had been turned upside down when her mother and her third husband were killed in an automobile accident, leaving her in the care of a half-sister she barely knew. At the time, Tj had been living in her own apartment in town and was involved in a semiserious romantic relationship with her boyfriend, Tyler. After Ashley, eight, and Gracie, five, came to live with her, she'd broken up with Tyler and moved back to the resort, where she had the help and support of her father, Mike, and Grandpa Ben. The first few months had been difficult, as everyone tried to adapt to the change in circumstances, but in the past few months, it had seemed like they'd turned a corner and settled down into a comfortable routine. She knew she needed to sit Ashley down and talk to her about channeling her anger into nonviolent outlets, but first she needed to deal with the impromptu meeting her boss had called just as she was getting ready to leave for the day.

Tj knocked on Greg Remington's office door. It seemed odd that he'd ask her to stop by when he knew she had downhill practice, but then again, Greg didn't always understand the importance of what it was she did for the school and the kids who had dreams of making it big in their sport of choice. To most of the kids on her downhill team, snowboarding was an after-school activity, but to serious boarders like Connor and Brittany, it was a future they had worked hard for their entire lives.

"Tj, have a seat," Greg instructed.

"If this is about the fight Ashley had with Loretta, I've already talked to Leslie," Tj said, attempting to head him off. Tj knew Greg tended to be a bit of a talker, but she figured the quicker they could get to the point of the conversation, the quicker she could get to the mountain and all that wonderful powder.

"This meeting isn't about Ashley and Loretta," Greg informed her. "I've spoken to both Leslie and Loretta's mother, and I believe we've come to an agreement."

"If this isn't about the fight, can whatever it is you'd like to discuss wait for another time? I have downhill practice," Tj reminded him. "The kids are already at the mountain. They'll be waiting."

Greg was a thirty-five-year-old transplant from a much larger school district in the Bay Area. He had big-city plans for their little school, and while Tj generally supported big dreams, it seemed at times that Greg's ideas translated into a bunch of extra work for her and the rest of the staff at the high school. The previous summer he'd hired a consultant to offer suggestions that would make them more viable in the competitive grant arena. One of the suggestions had been that the school offer more extracurricular activities in order to diversify their offerings, resulting in mandatory adjunct duty for all certified teachers. Tj had messed around, and by the time she'd gotten around to picking her adjunct duty, the choir had been all that was left. Eventually, she'd grown to enjoy her adjunct duty, but initially she'd been less than happy with the assignment.

"I'll make this quick. I guess you've heard that Travis Davidson is in town for the winter carnival." Greg ran his hand through his thick brown hair in a nervous gesture.

Tj shrugged. "Yeah. So?"

Travis might be a big shot to the downhill community as a whole, but here in his hometown, he was regarded as more of a snake. When Travis had grown up in Serenity, he'd been a young man with oodles of talent but a lack of resources. Local promoter Barney Johnson, who everyone just called Johnson, had taken him under his wing, lined up sponsors, hired him a private coach, and helped him follow his dream. Travis had promised his coach and sponsors that if he made it big, they'd all make it big. After winning last year's X Games, it looked like his dream of going pro might become a reality. The problem was, fame had gone to his head, and he'd quickly dumped the people who had gotten him where he was today.

"It seems that after his exceptional showing at the X Games, Mayor Wallaby has decided to make him the master of ceremonies for the winter carnival opening event. One of his stipulations for accepting the honor was that he be given creative freedom over the entire process."

"Creative freedom?"

"In a nutshell, he wants to have input in the songs your group will be performing."

"You can't be serious." Tj's blue eyes flashed in annoyance. The guy wins a couple of downhill events and suddenly he's telling her what to do? "We've been practicing for months. The opening ceremonies are in less than two weeks. There's no way we have time to change anything at this point."

"I understand your dilemma, but Mayor Wallaby insisted that you meet with Travis to discuss the matter. I set up a meeting for you tomorrow, during your prep period. I'm sure with your persuasive skills you can convince Mr. Davidson that the songs you've prepared will work just fine."

Tj got up from her chair and began to pace back and forth across the room. "The guy blows into town at the last minute and expects everyone to bow down to his ridiculous demands." Tj was a tiny thing at five foot two, but she had a reputation for being a redheaded spitfire when someone crossed her or someone she cared about. "The kids have spent hours perfecting their acts. They've poured their hearts and souls into creating something spectacular. There's no way I'm going to ask them to make any changes at this point."

"I'm just asking you to talk to him," Greg pleaded. "Go to the meeting and convince him to go with the songs you already have picked out."

"I'll talk to him all right." Tj stormed out of the room.

CHAPTER 2

By the time Tj finished working with her downhill team, the snowstorm had intensified to a blizzard. Driving slowly through the tiny alpine town, she was thankful for the extra illumination provided by the thousands of white lights draped in every tree and wrapped around every doorway and window on the north side of Main Street. The normally busy two-lane road was mostly deserted in spite of the fact that the clock on her dashboard indicated it was just a few minutes after six. Serenity, originally founded to support a large lumber operation, now boasted a charming downtown district consisting of a single main street lined on one side by Paradise Lake and on the other by a myriad of cozy shops displaying their wares in artfully decorated windows. The downtown strip was bordered to the north by a narrow stone bridge built more than seventy years earlier to allow a dry crossing of the Paradise River and to the south by a recently developed community park where summer concerts and local events like the annual snowman building competition were held.

Turning into the parking area behind the Antiquery, the cafe/antique store owned by her best friend, Jenna Elston, with her mother, Helen, and mother-in-law, Bonnie, Tj pulled up behind the back door leading from the kitchen to the alley. During the summer, visitors from the beach across the street were lined up out of the door from opening to closing, but during the off-season, the place felt more like a gathering in someone's kitchen, where locals congregated in booths, sharing a meal and discussing the latest news. The coffee shop served both breakfast and lunch but closed at three p.m., affording Jenna time to spend with her family. More often than not, however, she could be found working in the cozy kitchen until well past dark.

"It's really coming down out there," Tj commented as she walked from the storm into the kitchen, where Jenna was baking something that smelled like heaven. She slipped off her boots and left them to dry near the rack Jenna had set up for just that purpose. Walking across the spotless tile floor in her wool socks, Tj slid onto one of the tall stools lining the counter. "Three feet and counting. If this keeps up, we're going to exceed the four feet the National Weather Service predicted."

Unlike many restaurants, the kitchen at the Antiquery was warm and inviting, with colorful accents and decorative touches. Large copper pots hung from wrought-iron hooks and baskets of seasonal fruits and vegetables were arranged on the green-tile countertops lining every wall of the large industrial space. While the appliances were commercial, the decor included cheery wallpaper and colorful curtains that were homey and welcoming.

"I'm betting there'll be a snow day tomorrow," Jenna replied as the strong wind rattled the ice-covered windows. "Dennis has a shift, so I guess I should talk to Bonnie about watching the girls."

Jenna's husband, Dennis, was a firefighter for the Paradise Lake Fire District. While his shifts comprised either thirty-six or forty-eight hours, he had a lot of time off between them and was often home to help out with their two daughters. When both parents were stuck at work, doting grandmothers Helen and Bonnie were ready and waiting to step in.

"Bring Kristi and Kari to the resort," Tj suggested. "I've already confirmed that Grandpa will be around to watch Ashley and Gracie. He won't mind a couple more. In fact, it's usually easier to have all four girls. They tend to keep one another entertained."

"Thanks. I might take you up on that." Jenna slid a cup of hot coffee across the counter to Tj. "If the schools are closed, it might be busy, and I could really use Bonnie's help here at the restaurant." Jenna pulled a tray of cookies out of the oven and set them on the cooling rack. "Want a cookie to go with that coffee?"

Tj hesitated. While her downhill team, in their youthful exuberance, had torn up the mountain with all the fresh powder, after spending several hours in the whiteout conditions, she was cold and wet and exhausted. What she really wanted was to go home and curl up by the fire with her Bernese mountain dog, Echo, and huge orange tabby, Cuervo, and drift into a dreamless sleep. On the other hand, something did smell awfully good, and she had a date that night, so an early bedtime was out of the question anyway.

"Chocolate oatmeal crisps hot out of the oven," Jenna encouraged as she put two on a plate and set it next to the coffee she'd poured. You can't be best friends with someone for twenty-three years and not know that they never turn down an offer of chocolate. "I changed up the recipe a bit and added just a bit of caramel. I think it gives an interesting twist to an old favorite."

Tj took a bite; it was delicious. In all of the excitement brought about by the new snow, she'd barely eaten at all that day.

"These are really good. Can I have a couple more and a glass of milk?"

Jenna piled four more cookies on the plate while Tj got her own glass of milk from the restaurant-sized refrigerator.

"Where are the girls?" Tj wondered.

Most afternoons, they could be found sitting at the table Jenna kept tucked into a corner of the kitchen doing their homework.

"Up front with Mom and Bonnie," Jenna answered. "Mom went to an estate sale last weekend and picked up a bunch of stuff from the turn of the century. She's completely redesigning the window display to accommodate her new pieces. Bonnie and the girls are helping."

Tj knew Helen was meticulous in her mission to buy the highest-quality antiques, then painstakingly restore them to their original magnificence. Each piece was grouped in a period exhibit in which scrupulous attention to detail provided for museum-quality displays.

"Ashley got into another fight today," Tj informed Jenna as she settled in with her snack.

"Oh no," Jenna sympathized as she began gathering ingredients for what looked like clam chowder. "She's been doing so well. What happened?"

"Loretta is having a birthday party. She invited the whole class with the exception of Ashley."

Jenna frowned. "That's mean. I can't believe her mom would let her do that. I know Kristi got an invite, but I'll talk to her about doing something fun with Ashley on the day of the party instead."

"That's really nice, but I don't want Kristi to miss the biggest party of the year just because Ashley wasn't included."

"I'll see how she feels about it," Jenna promised. "My guess is that she won't want to go after she hears that Ashley wasn't invited, but I'll leave the decision up to her."

"Kyle and I have been talking about taking the girls to the Children's Museum in Carson City," Tj informed Jenna. "Maybe we'll do it on the day of Loretta's party. Kristi and Kari are both invited if they want to go. Having something fun to do should take Ashley's mind off the fact that she wasn't included in the biggest social event on the third-grade calendar."

"Sounds fun." Jenna smiled. "How did Kyle do with the choir?"

"Kyle did great but you'll never guess who wants to have input about the music my kids will perform for the carnival opening ceremonies."

"Who?"

"Travis Davidson. I guess he's acting as some sort of honorary master of ceremonies. One of his conditions for accepting the gig was that he wanted to be given creative control over the entire ceremony, including which songs my group will perform."

"Wow, really? The kids have been rehearsing for months." Jenna had been a steadfast supporter of Tj and her attempt to convert the misfits into a choir. "There's no way there's enough time to change things at this point."

"Tell me about it. I've been fuming since I found out about the ridiculous request. Greg seems to think that if I meet with Travis and explain things, he'll understand our predicament. I agreed to meet with him, but if I know Travis the way I think I know him, he'll demand changes just to be an ass."

"Don't let Travis push your buttons," Jenna counseled. "I know the two of you have never gotten along, but it seems like he has a tendency to bring out the worst in you."

"I know, but he's just so..." Several adjectives came to mind, none of them appropriate for polite company. As far as Tj was concerned, Travis was an arrogant cuss who came to the community for help when he needed it and then dumped the people who cared about him when he got a better offer. Tj had convinced her dad to put up a considerable amount of money to back him, only to be told that his sponsorship was no longer needed once Travis had become a name on the pro circuit. Travis didn't deserve the consideration the mayor appeared to be granting him.

"I realize that my problems with Travis are my problems, and I know I can't let my personal feelings get in the way of making sure the toad doesn't ruin the show the kids have poured their heart and soul into," Tj continued. "But if that guy thinks he can waltz into town and mess with *my* choir, he has another thing coming."

Jenna smiled. "You know, that's the first time you've referred to the kids as *your* choir with quite so much ownership. They've gotten to you in spite of the fact that you didn't want anything to do with the group in the beginning."

"Yeah. I'll admit I fought the assignment when Greg first approached me with it, but the kids are really awesome. They deserve this chance to shine and I don't want Travis messing with it."

"What are you going to do?"

"My gut tells me I should just wring the guy's scrawny neck and be done with it. But I guess I'll pretend to be the responsible adult everyone seems to think I should be and have a chat with him, as Greg requested. I assume we'll still meet even if school is canceled."

"Talking is good. The last thing we need is for the famous Tj temper to make things worse. I'm actually kind of surprised the guy came back to town," Jenna added. "He ticked off a lot of people when he left. I'm betting you aren't the only one who would love to wring his neck."

Tj glanced out of the kitchen window as heavy snow pelted the side of the building. "Mayor Wallaby thinks he's some kind of local hero. From what I hear, the carnival committee wasn't even informed about the invitation until after Travis and his new agent had already signed the contract for him to appear. I guess a lot of the committee members were upset, but Wallaby is insisting that our little event needs a national spotlight and Travis is just the one to give it to us."

"I get why Wallaby might want Travis to attend the event, but what I don't understand is why Travis agreed to come."

"The guy has a huge ego." Tj grabbed two more cookies off the cooling rack. "Wallaby is going all out to feed that ego and make him feel welcome. There's even going to be a reception of some type up at the lodge. As a coach for a high-school team I got an invite, but I'm seriously disinclined to go."

"Does Chelsea know he's back?" Jenna asked.

Chelsea was Tj's ex-boyfriend Hunter Hanson's sister.

"She must. Everyone is talking about it."

"After he dumped her for that Swedish supermodel, I thought she was going to kill him. They dated for a long time."

"I thought I'd text her later, see if she needs talking down. Not that the punk doesn't deserve whatever he gets, but Chelsea really doesn't have the coloring to pull off an orange jumpsuit."

Jenna laughed.

Tj took a last sip of her coffee. "I guess I should round up the girls and get home. Dylan's picking me up in just over an hour, and I still have to get cleaned up."

"Another date that's not a date?"

"Yeah, something like that. New movie at the fourplex."

Dylan Caine, the new deputy in town, wasn't only a total

babe and a fantastic guy Tj found herself more than a little attracted to; he was also a man with a tragic past who obviously wasn't ready to date an overencumbered schoolteacher or anyone else. While Tj would be open to moving their relationship to the next level, she was content for the time being to enjoy the friendship they'd established over the past few months.

Jenna's mother, Helen Henderson, dressed in a smart olive-green suit, pushed her way in though the kitchen door with Jenna's mother-in-law, Bonnie Elston, Ashley, Gracie, and Jenna's daughters, Kristi and Kari, on her heels. Helen, a petite green-eyed brunette, was the self-appointed queen bee of the Serenity gossip hive and therefore the frequent recipient of visits from locals with the current buzz.

"You'll never guess who just stopped by. Barney Johnson," Bonnie answered her own question before either Tj or Jenna could speak.

"He's circulating a petition to replace Travis with a local athlete as celebrity guest for the carnival," Helen added.

"Wallaby's never going to go for it," Jenna speculated as she put cookies on a plate and poured four glasses of milk for the girls.

"He won't have a choice if Johnson can get the support he needs. I heard Travis has a sponsorship deal riding on his ability to expand his public exposure. The whole reason he agreed to be honorary master of ceremonies was to impress this potential funding source. Johnson thinks it's a slap in the face to the local folks who contributed their hard-earned dollars to launch his career in the first place only to be shunted aside the minute he made it big."

"According to Harriet, Wallaby is livid," Bonnie said, referring to Harriet Kramer, Mayor Wallaby's busybody secretary. "He's threatening to have Johnson kicked off the town council if he doesn't drop the petition."

"Can he do that?" Tj asked.

"Not really," Bonnie admitted, "but he can make life difficult if he chooses. Johnson is trying to expand his feed store, and Wallaby is chair of the committee to review the project."

Tj frowned. "I doubt the mayor would use his influence with the committee over something as minor as a celebrity master of ceremonies."

"Harriet thinks there's more going on than meets the eye," Bonnie supplied. "She indicated—in strictest confidence, of course—that Wallaby might have ulterior motives for getting in bed with the toad."

"Ulterior motives?" Tj wondered.

"Harriet didn't have many details, but while she was doing filing in the storage room next to Wallaby's office, she happened to overhear the men talking about some sort of a deal."

Tj rolled her eyes. Harriet was famous for filing at opportune moments.

"What sort of deal?" Tj asked.

"Harriet didn't know for certain," Bonnie said, "but if she had to bet on it, she'd guess that there are large amounts of money involved. Harriet thinks Wallaby is getting some type of payoff in exchange for helping Travis get the sponsorship he's going after."

Tj thought about what Bonnie had shared. She certainly wouldn't put it past Wallaby to stoop to something so low. Not that the guy was a crook, but in the ten years he'd served the good people of Serenity, this wouldn't be the first time he'd made an official decision based on the potential for personal gain.

Tj knew that his wife had kicked him out over the Christmas holiday after finding out he'd been "keeping company" with a wealthy widow in the neighboring town of Indulgence. The local rumor mill had indicated that she planned to take him for everything he had and then some. The chance at a large payout to help fund his depleted bank account was probably more than he could resist.

"Grandpa told me the council is kicking around the idea of sponsoring another candidate for mayor next fall," Tj informed the group. "I guess they've finally had enough of his questionable behavior."

"Wallaby's been mayor for a decade," Helen pointed out. "Does the council think they have someone who can defeat him?"

"I don't know," Tj admitted as she poured herself another cup of coffee. "I'm pretty sure it's all talk at this point."

"Let's face it, the majority of the town's citizens don't give a hoot about local politics and will vote for the familiar over the unfamiliar any day of the week," Bonnie interjected. "They'd have to get someone who was already well known and respected to have a chance of beating Wallaby."

After they returned to Maggie's Hideaway, the resort her father owned, Tj pulled Ashley into her room so they could have a private conversation.

The house where the Jensen family lived was a large two-story log structure with the living space on the first floor and the bedrooms on the second. Tj's room was at the end of the hall, overlooking the lake. "I talked to Ms. Grayson this afternoon," Tj began.

Ashley paled.

Tj sat down on the edge of her bed and pulled her sister down beside her. "Do you want to tell me what happened?"

Ashley started to cry. "I know you told me I shouldn't hit people, but I just got so mad," she sobbed. "Stupid Loretta was bragging to everyone about her stupid party during recess. I asked her if I could come too and she said I was a stupid head and not invited."

"Do you know why she didn't invite you?" Tj asked as she held her sister in her arms.

"'Cause I pushed her in the camel poop," Ashley admitted. "But she was saying mean things about Mom. She deserved to get pushed."

Tj agreed but didn't say as much. What kind of mother let her daughter invite everyone in the class to a party with the exception of one student? If Loretta's mom wasn't careful, she was going to find herself on the other end of Tj's temper, and that never worked out well for anyone.

"Are you mad?" Ashley asked.

Tj hesitated. She knew it was important to say the right thing now and in all honesty, she wasn't sure what that was. She sympathized with Ashley and didn't blame her for hitting Loretta, but her sister was going to come into contact with a lot of mean and rude people in her life, and she couldn't go around assaulting all of them.

"I'm not mad," Tj stroked Ashley's hair, "but I am concerned. I know that sometimes people are so mean to us that we want to hit them, but we have to be mature enough to know that hitting isn't a good solution to our problems."

"What *is* a good solution?"

Good question. Tj had to admit she wasn't exactly known for keeping her cool when someone angered her.

"Honestly," Tj wiped the tears from her sister's face, then

looked her directly in the eye, "I'm not sure. I know that most adults will tell you to ignore people who are mean to you, to walk away rather than fight back, but I know sometimes doing that can be really hard. I'm afraid that both of us were born with fiery tempers to go with our red hair."

Ashley smiled.

"Mrs. Remington is going to meet with us later this week. She's been trained to help people like us deal with bullies. Maybe she can give us *both* some tips."

"Okay." Ashley hugged her big sister.

"In the meantime, you'll need to spend your recess inside with Ms. Grayson. I don't want you to give her a bad time about it. It's not her fault you got detention."

"I know. I'll be nice. I promise."

Tj smiled. "I love you, you know."

"I know." Ashley smiled back. "I love you too."

CHAPTER 3

Tuesday, February 11

Tj tried to move, but she was trapped between immovable objects weighing down her arms and legs. She could hear the ringing in the background and knew she needed to fight toward consciousness if she was to stop the incessant clatter. Struggling to open her eyes, she was greeted by total darkness. Fighting to unwind her limbs from the mass of animals littering her bed, she reached for the cell phone she'd left on her bedside table and pushed the answer button. The last thing she wanted to do was wake up the entire household at—she glanced at the clock—six a.m.

"Hello," she said groggily.

"This is a recorded announcement. All schools in Paradise County are closed due to snow." As Tj listened to the familiar recording, she frowned. If school was closed for the day, did they have to call *quite* so early? Given the amount of snow that had fallen during the previous twenty-four hours, everyone at the lake must have assumed there would be a snow day before they even went to bed. Why not officially call it then and let everyone sleep in?

Tj tried to go back to sleep, but the beasts surrounding her had been awakened. She could feel her dog's hot breath caressing her face as her cat began rhythmically massaging her arm with his sharp claws. "Just another hour," she pleaded.

Echo, her one-hundred-thirty-pound Bernese mountain dog, politely and obediently laid back down, but Cuervo, the huge orange tomcat, who was neither obedient nor polite, pounced on her head as she rolled over and tried to close her eyes. Cuervo was a difficult cat who liked to call the shots and rarely took no for an answer. He wasn't sweet and cuddly, like Gracie's cat, Crissy, and on more than one occasion he'd demonstrated a propensity for using his claws when he was displeased. But in spite of his fractious nature, Tj loved him.

"Okay, okay, I'm getting up." Tj shivered as she pulled back the heavy down comforter. She pulled a long sweatshirt over the flannels she slept in before slipping her feet into her knee-high slippers.

Dragging herself into the bathroom, she brushed her teeth and pulled her long mass of auburn curls into a sloppy knot on the top of her head. Heading down the hall, she could hear laughter coming from the kitchen below.

"Morning, everyone," Tj greeted as she poured a cup of coffee from the pot on the dark green counter.

"Snow day!" Ashley and Gracie cheered as Tj slid onto one of the tall stools positioned around the kitchen counter. Tj took a long sip of her coffee and stared out of the window at the lake beyond.

The blowing wind obscured the normally priceless view, but the effect of the stormy day combined with the warm and cozy kitchen left her feeling happy and content in spite of the long day ahead.

"I hope it's okay that I told Jenna she could bring Kristi and

Kari over," she informed her grandpa, who was standing behind the eight-burner stove.

"More the merrier." Ben smiled as he stirred something that smelled like bacon sizzling in the large cast-iron skillet.

"Kristi and Kari are coming?" Ashley asked. "Can we make cupcakes? The last time they were here, you said we could make cupcakes next time," she reminded her older sister.

Tj groaned. She *had* said that. If there was one thing she still needed to learn about being a mother—or, in her case, a mother substitute—it was not to make promises you might not be able to keep.

"I'm not sure I'll have time. I need to meet with Travis Davidson about the opening ceremony, and I promised Papa I'd take care of some errands while I'm in town."

"I can help the girls with the cupcakes," Ben offered.

"Really? That would be great."

"Been thinking about doing some baking, and today seems as good a day as any. How about some pancakes to go with that coffee?"

"Yeah, thanks." Tj didn't always have time for a big breakfast, but with the snow pelting the window and the warmth from the cozy brick fireplace, it seemed like a pancakes kind of day.

"Blueberry or regular?"

"Regular," Tj replied before helping herself to a second cup of the liquid adrenaline her grandfather had brewed. "Where's Dad?"

"Plowing," her grandpa said. Ben was tall and rugged, with snowy white hair and a beckoning smile that pulled you in like a warm embrace. Thick wool socks were topped with faded blue jeans and a royal-blue sweater that perfectly matched his eyes. "The snow is a welcome event, but it's going to be a busy week."

"It's only Tuesday, and most of the guests aren't scheduled to arrive until Friday," Tj pointed out. "The National Weather Service says the storm should pass by tomorrow evening, so we should get everything dug out before the bulk of the guests arrive."

"Hope they're right." Ben slid three golden pancakes onto a plate. "Bacon?"

"Yeah, thanks."

"Me and Ashley entered a contest," Gracie informed Tj.

"What kind of contest?" Tj poured homemade maple syrup over her golden stack.

"A snowman contest," Ashley supplied.

"For the winter carnival?" Tj clarified.

"Yeah, we're going to make a big one." Gracie's long ringlets of dark hair bobbed up and down as she fidgeted with excitement.

"With clothes and everything." Ashley's green eyes shone bright with excitement as she jumped out of her chair and began twirling around. "Grandpa says we're going to have the best darn snowman this side of the Rockies."

"Grandpa is going to help you?"

"Yeah, he said you'd be busy."

"Unfortunately, Grandpa is right." Tj felt bad that she wouldn't be available to help the girls build their snowman, but her downhill event was scheduled for the same time as the snowman competition. "I'm really sorry I won't be able to help you build it, but I'll be there for the judging."

"It's okay." Ashley shrugged as she tucked a lock of strawberry-blond hair behind one ear. "Grandpa told us he's a snowman-building expert."

"I'm sure he is."

"The carnival is going to be so fun." Ashley bounced around the room. "Everyone is doing something. Me and Gracie are building a snowman and Grandpa is entering the ice fishing."

"And Papa is going to dance with Rosalie," Gracie added before Ashley could finish.

"I was going to say that," Ashley complained.

"Dance with Rosalie?" Tj asked. Rosalie was her father Mike's "not a girlfriend" in much the way that Dylan was her "not a boyfriend."

"At the carnival," Ashley clarified. "When we told him we were entering the snowman competition, he told us that he was entering the ice-dancing competition with Rosalie."

"Are you sure he said ice dancing?" Tj had never seen her dad partake of any type of dancing, and he certainly didn't seem the type to enter an ice-dancing competition.

Ashley laughed. "I thought it was funny too, but he said Miss Rosalie asked real nice and he couldn't say no. He said he's been practicing."

Tj looked at her grandpa, who had joined the group with his own plate of pancakes. "Did you know about this?"

"Mike might have mentioned it a time or two."

"And you think he's serious? I mean, maybe he was kidding." Tj decided that made a lot more sense. As hard as she tried, she couldn't imagine her rugged father skating around Miller's Pond to the beat of classical music. "That's it; he must have been kidding."

"Didn't seem like he was kidding," Ben said.

"But ice dancing?"

"Aunt Jenna is entering the baking contest, Kristi and Kari are doing ice skating, and Uncle Dennis is going to ride a dog." Gracie frowned as she tried to work the image out in her mind.

"He's not riding a dog, he's riding in a sled pulled by a dog," Ashley clarified. "Are you going to do a contest?"

"Well," Tj hesitated, "I'm not really entering a contest directly, but I'm coaching a team that's entering a contest."

"That doesn't count," Ashley argued. "You need to enter something that's just for you."

"I'll be pretty busy with the downhill team," Tj explained.

"That's during the day." Ashley wasn't giving up. "You can enter something at night."

"I don't think they have competitions at night."

"Papa said the ice dancing is at night." Ashley was like a dog with a bone when she got an idea in her head.

"Yeah, but I couldn't compete against Papa."

Ashley began kicking the leg of the table, causing the whole thing to wobble as she considered her options. Tj felt bad that she was the only member of the family not participating, but she really was too busy to build a snowman, dance around a pond, or pluck fish from a hole in the ice. Her downhill team was scheduled to compete in a series of events during the first two days of the four-day event. Maybe she could enter one of the contests slated for the weekend. There were snowmobile races, snowshoe competitions, and ice-climbing demonstrations, all events she'd been involved in during years past.

"I think the ice-princess thing is at night," Gracie suggested.

"God, no," Tj spat without thinking. She regretted her outburst when she noticed giant tears well up in Gracie's eyes. "I mean, I'm very flattered that you think I'm beautiful enough to be the ice princess, but I'm pretty sure it's for younger girls. Much, much younger," she emphasized.

"But..." Gracie began.

"Perhaps you could enter the snowball decathlon," Ben suggested. "It's on the final day of the carnival, so you should be done with your team events by then."

Tj shot Ben a look of gratitude. "I could do that."

"What's a snowball cathlon?" Gracie asked.

"It's a series of events utilizing snowballs," Tj explained. "There's one event in which you fling a snowball at a target using a sling shot and are scored on accuracy. There's another similar event in which the object is to propel your snowball over the longest distance. In all, there are usually five different events. Each one is scored individually, and whoever ends up with the highest overall score wins."

"Okay." Gracie smiled.

"Kristi's here." Ashley jumped up and ran down the hall at the sound of the doorbell. Gracie followed closely behind as Ben's friends Doc and Bookman stomped snow from their feet. Each of the men carried a blond-haired child in his arms.

"Here yah go, little darling." Doc, a retired coroner and local Casanova for the senior population, set Kari on the floor. "Delivered safe and sound, just like I promised your mama."

"How come you carried Kristi and Kari to the house?" Gracie asked as Bookman set Kristi down next to Kari and Tj helped the girls remove their boots and hang up their coats.

"The snow is so deep, I was afraid I'd lose these little munchkins between the car and the house."

"I thought I was going to pick up the girls." Tj hung the backpacks the girls had been carrying on hooks near the door.

"We stopped by the Antiquery for some breakfast," Bookman explained. "Helen mentioned that the girls were going to spend the day at the resort. We were coming out anyway, so we offered to deliver the girls. Jenna said she texted you."

Tj hadn't thought to check her messages. "Yeah, she probably did."

"Let's go upstairs." Ashley grabbed Kristi's arm and led her to her bedroom, with Gracie and Kari trailing behind.

"I appreciate your bringing the girls." Tj hugged the men,

who were more like honorary uncles than mere friends. "I have to go into town later, but now I can take my time getting ready."

"That new plow driver the county hired seems to think the snow goes in the middle of the road," Bookman informed her. "Best take the truck if you're headin' out."

"Yeah, I will. How about some coffee?"

"You read my mind." Doc gave her a hug as they headed back toward the kitchen. "Something smells good."

"We had bacon for breakfast, plus Grandpa's making soup. Navy bean with ham."

"There's nothing better than the smell of soup simmering on the stove on a stormy day." Doc opened the lid to take a peek, while Tj poured the men cups of coffee. "I guess you heard that the carnival committee decided not to let anyone with a retail eatery enter the chowder contest this year."

"Jenna mentioned it," Tj confirmed.

"With Jenna out of the running, I thought I'd throw my hat in the ring," Doc announced. "I've been working on a recipe."

"I definitely think you should enter. Ashley pointed out that everyone in the family is entering an event. I wasn't going to bother entering anything at first, but she guilted me into agreeing to enter the snowball decathlon. How about it, Bookman? Anything you might be interested in?"

"I already entered the toboggan race with Helen."

"Helen entered the toboggan race?" Every year, teams of one man and one woman flew down Daredevil Hill on two-man toboggans designed and built by the competing team. Most of the participants were high-school students as part of a science project.

As far as Tj knew, Helen and Bookman would be the only team with a combined age exceeding the century mark ever to brave the hill.

"Yeah," Bookman confirmed. "I was surprised when she asked me to partner with her, but she seems excited about the whole thing. We've been spending every night in my garage working on the sled for weeks now."

Ah, Tj thought. Two weeks of working alone with Bookman at his beautiful lakeside estate. Tj suddenly realized the reason Helen might suddenly have developed an interest in downhill propulsion.

CHAPTER 4

Bookman's comment about the new plow driver was an understatement, Tj decided. Not only were more than half of the roads still unplowed by the time she made it into Serenity, but the roads that were plowed had a huge berm in the middle, making it impossible to make a left-hand turn. After driving at least two miles out of her way, she found a place where she could turn around and head back toward the town she had just driven through. She supposed she could have parked on the lakeside of the road and climbed over the berm to get to the shops on the other side, but with her luck, some idiot would speed by just as she reached the apex of the slush pile and douse her with muddy sludge from the road.

Thankfully, most of the town's patrons had taken care of removing the snow from the parking areas near their business establishments. As long as she did her errands in a linear fashion, there shouldn't be a need to cross back over the highway. The snow was still falling by the time she reached her first destination, although the intensity had diminished greatly. If the local weather report was correct, the storm should pass by the next day, bringing sun to the region for the foreseeable future.

"Morning, Hazel," Tj greeted Hazel Whipple, the seventy-two-year-old postmistress who everyone thought should have retired a generation earlier. Hazel was tall and regal in spite of her age. Roller-curled white hair topped a perfectly groomed frame, right down to the polished leather shoes that peeked daintily from the perfectly pressed housedress that hung to a point just above her ankles.

"Wipe those boots before you walk across my floor," Hazel warned.

"Yes, ma'am, I will." Tj stomped all the snow from her shoes, then wiped them several times on the carpet just inside the door. "My dad said he has a package."

Hazel slid a small box across the counter. "Seems like this is the third seal your dad has ordered for that old pump of yours in as many months. Not that it's any of my business, but it seems that it might be prudent to just buy a new pump."

"You could be right. I'll mention it to Dad." Hazel was famous for offering unsolicited advice with every serving of mail. Most folks in town shrugged off her suggestions without taking offense, but every now and then Hazel poked her nose in where it really didn't belong and Mayor Wallaby had to smooth ruffled feathers on behalf of the town.

"I'm surprised Mike didn't pick up the seal himself. He mentioned he'd stop by and take me to lunch the last time I ran into him at Grainger's," Hazel said, referring to the general store.

"It's been pretty hectic with the carnival just around the corner. And the snow, while welcome, has added a whole other set of chores to his already heavy load. I'm sure he'll be by after we get through the carnival crush."

"Seems like the carnival is adding to everyone's burden this year." Hazel adjusted the wire-framed glasses on her weathered face. "Guess you heard about our Chelsea."

"Something happened to Chelsea?"

"That no-good ex of hers had the nerve to show up at book club and make a scene. I can't repeat the exact words he used because I'm a lady and not prone to repeating such language. I can say, however, that our little Chelsea turned an unfortunate shade of red. The poor girl was beyond mortified. I swear, if she had a weapon, the boy would be sliced and toasted."

"He seems to have that effect on people."

"In my day, gentlemen had respect for the fairer sex. If they had a beef with someone they once dated, they kept it to themselves."

"So what did Chelsea do?" Tj knew that Chelsea Hanson was no damsel in distress. If Travis got in her face, you'd better bet that she'd be all up in his in return.

"She grabbed the rude young man by the arm and walked him out of the door. I'm not sure what happened after that. Neither of them returned. A friend offered to take Chelsea's coat and purse to her once we finished our meeting."

"Personally, I think the addition of Travis to the mix adds an element of stress to an already busy event." Tj liked to think she was above gossip, but the truth of the matter was, she was as apt to get pulled into a rant as the next woman. "I can't imagine what Mayor Wallaby was thinking when he invited Travis to participate."

"I've heard the scuttlebutt about the mayor's involvement," Hazel informed her. "Harriet seems to think the mayor isn't above accepting a payoff, and I have to say I'm inclined to agree. Why, just last week, Wallaby's wife served him with official divorce papers, and for the past three months, most of his utility bills have been marked as delinquent. If you ask me, the man is in a financial pickle, and I'm betting it started long before his wife moved in with her sister."

"Yes, well, I guess we'll see."

Tj realized she was dangerously close to getting pulled into a conversation based on pure speculation. After chatting a bit longer, Tj continued to the mayor's office on foot. She wasn't looking forward to her chat with the man-child who had the community in such an uproar, but she'd promised Greg Remington she'd try to reason with the idiot, so reason with him she would.

"Hey, Harriet," Tj greeted Mayor Wallaby's secretary. "I'm here for my mayor-mandated meeting with the town snake."

Harriet laughed. "I'm afraid the golden boy hasn't shown up yet. Wallaby is on the phone. Care for a cup of coffee?"

"I'd love one."

Tj sat down on one of the straight-backed chairs lining the waiting area. The office was small, with a reception area, just one interior office, and a storage room. The walls, carpet, and curtains were brown, giving the place a dark and oppressive feel. Harriet complained about the decor on a weekly basis, but apparently, Mayor Wallaby liked brown and refused to make any changes.

"Quite a storm that blew in." Harriet poured herself a cup of coffee, then sat down next to Tj.

"Are you talking about the snow or the snowboarder?"

"Both, actually." Harriet leaned in close. Everyone in town knew she was the second-biggest gossip in the county next to Helen. "The phones have been ringing all day with unhappy residents complaining about Mr. Davidson's behavior. Murphy called to say that Travis started a fight in his bar resulting in several hundred dollars' worth of damage, and Albert Pitman over at the Angel Mountain Inn complained that Travis had a steady parade of women coming and going all night, disturbing his other guests."

"Why didn't Murphy call the sheriff and Albert kick the bum out?"

Harriet looked toward the mayor's closed door before she answered in a whisper. "Everyone knows that Travis is here as the mayor's special guest. Wallaby is a regular patron of Murphy's bar, so Murphy wanted to give the man a chance to fix things without involving the sheriff, and Albert said the mayor was footing the bill for Travis's stay and didn't want to risk his refusing to pay if he kicked the guy out. I guess the mayor booked the Summit Suite, and the bill for Travis's three-week stay promises to be quite a doozy. He figured the mayor could talk to Travis, maybe convince him to act like a civilized human being."

"And did he? Square things with Murphy and Albert, I mean?"

"Nope. He simply explained that Travis's appearance at the carnival was bringing national attention to the town and we had to expect to put up with an eccentricity or two from such a big name."

Harriet stopped talking as the door separating the waiting area from the mayor's private office opened. "Tj, I'm sorry to keep you waiting." Tj noticed that the mayor's chubby face was an odd shade of red brought on, she imagined, by a high level of stress. "I'm afraid Travis won't be meeting with us after all. Apparently, he's been detained."

"Fantastic." Tj stood up. She was more than happy to avoid a confrontation with the jerk. "I'll be on my way."

"Uh…" The mayor looked at the floor. "Travis did have a few suggestions, which he asked me to pass on."

"Suggestions?"

Mayor Wallaby handed her a piece of notepaper. On the white page was a list of songs. "He would like your choir to sing songs from this playlist."

"With all due respect," Tj said, looking the mayor directly in the eye, "there's no way in hell I'm changing the playlist at this late date. If *Mr.* Davidson has a problem with that, he knows where to find me."

"But, Tj..." Mayor Wallaby began. Tj glared at the pudgy man across the room. He actually broke out in a sweat, even though the temperature in the office couldn't be more than sixty degrees. Travis might think he was pulling the mayor's strings, but Tj could stare down a grizzly if she had to.

"No way in hell," she reiterated before stomping out of the office.

CHAPTER 5

Friday, February 14

"First of all, I want to congratulate everyone on their efforts this afternoon." Tj huddled around her downhill team in the warming hut provided for their use by Angel Mountain Ski Resort. "Beaver Creek has a slight edge over us in overall points this season, but Connor has the most individual points among the boys in the slalom and Brittany is dominating the girls in all categories. If we want to maintain our position going into regionals, we're going to need a strong showing next weekend. Eric, you're up first on Thursday and will need a time of at least 2:15:14 to gain position in the rankings."

"I'm ready," Eric Weldy, a senior and Tj's second-best male snowboarder, assured her. "I've had strong runs all week and feel like I can set a personal record, but I wish we were doing our runs in the morning rather than the afternoon."

"The carnival committee decided to start things off with demonstrations by the professional boarders," Tj explained. "According to my schedule, Travis Davidson is slated to take the hill at eleven, followed by Sean Wright. Our first event is scheduled immediately after that."

"I heard Travis was peeved the committee invited Sean to the event," Connor informed the group. "Guess the two don't get along."

"Sean's gaining ground in the world rankings," Tj added. "If Sean continues to post wins the way he has been lately, Travis is going to have to get used to sharing the spotlight."

"Dude's a total prima donna," Gary Paulson, a freshman and new team member, replied. "Guy's never gonna get used to sharing the spotlight."

"Like you know anything about Travis," Sarah Blakely, also a senior, defended. "The guy's legit. He shouldn't have to share."

"Yeah, what would you know?" Gary shot back.

"Travis and I have spent some time together since he's been in town," Sarah bragged. "He was friends with my sister when he lived here. We met up at the lodge and he asked about her, so we've been hanging."

"A little too much," her boyfriend Eric muttered under his breath.

"Okay, let's get back to the subject at hand." Based on the fire in Eric's eye, Tj decided it was best to steer the conversation away from Travis Davidson. One of the reasons Tj frowned on romantic relationships between team members was because when things went bad—and they inevitably did between high schoolers—the entire team suffered from the fallout. Last year, Jilli Smith had dated a senior who had since moved on to college. When the relationship imploded, Tj had been subjected to months of bickering as members of the team took sides in the dispute. While they did well in regionals, Tj suspected they would have done even better if they'd come to the competition with a united front.

Turning her attention to her second-best female boarder, she asked, "So Jilli, how's the knee holding up?"

"It feels good. I've been wearing the brace the doctor gave me, but I feel like it interferes with my timing. I'm thinking about ditching it when we get to the competition."

"As your coach, I am indisputably telling you not to ditch the brace. You may be off your personal best, but your times are good, and we wouldn't want to risk another injury."

"Okay."

Tj knew Jilli was disappointed that her knee was holding her back, but the last thing she needed to do was risk a much more serious injury. Tj had seen too many careers destroyed before they ever got started due to an overzealous rehab schedule.

"Let's go over our schedule for tomorrow, and then you're all free to go home and get a good night's sleep."

"Aw, come on, Coach," Gary whined. "It's the weekend *and* Valentine's Day. There are a couple of parties around town. A bunch of us were planning to hang, maybe try to pick up depressed girls who find themselves dateless on the ultimate date night."

"We're meeting at the base of Grizzly Run at nine," Tj reminded him. "If you use up all your energy 'hanging,' you'll be worthless tomorrow."

"Coach is right," Connor added. "We can party after we win this thing."

"Look who's a teacher's pet," Gary teased.

"Dude, I have a scholarship on the line. My parents don't have the bank yours do. If I don't get a free ride, I'm working for my dad in the grocery store."

"I agree with Connor," Brittany chimed in. "I need a free ride as badly as he does, and we need your help to get the points, so how about it?"

"Yeah, okay," everyone muttered.

Tj knew she'd made a good choice when she'd made Connor and Brittany team captains. Not only were they the strongest athletes but they had the respect of the entire team, and more often than not, were able to make headway when Tj couldn't. She was going to miss them both when they graduated and went off to college.

Being a teacher inevitably meant annual goodbyes, but over the years there had been a few students who managed to worm their way into Tj's heart just a bit more than the others.

By the time the county plow service had finished clearing the roads, walls of snow almost six feet in height lined the narrow mountain road connecting Maggie's Hideaway, on the west bank of Paradise Lake, to the town of Serenity to the north. As Tj turned onto the private road leading up to the resort, she slowed to navigate the icy conditions. Making a slight right-hand turn toward the lodge, she swerved to avoid a pair of coyotes that had run in front of her and then disappeared behind the embankment.

She slowed as she made her way through the village, which consisted of a general store, an ice-cream shop, a bike and ski rental shop, and a single-pump gas station. If you included the marina and horse stable, Maggie's Hideaway was the largest resort on Paradise Lake.

Parking her 4Runner near the back service entrance, she pulled on her fuzzy blue mittens and stepped out into the clear night air. There was nothing quite as beautiful as the night sky after a storm. Billions of stars twinkled brightly as the moon shone down on the glassy lake beyond the lodge. Accessing the lodge through the back door, she passed through the administration office and entered the reception area. The building, designed by her grandfather more than forty years ago, was fashioned from logs cut and milled on the property. The main room of the lodge featured a river-rock fireplace reaching more than two stories in height. The mantel, which her grandfather had carved by hand, housed tin oil lamps that flickered in time to the flames from the real wood fire burning below. While the main lounge was open to the second floor, the office space at the back of the building was covered by cozy rooms with a mountain decor overlooking the lake beyond.

Tj poured herself a cup of coffee before scanning the arrival log, which someone had left lying on the shiny wood counter. It was well past six, and most of the arrivals had either retired to their rooms or the Lakeside Bar and Grill for dinner or a cocktail. In all, six of their guests remained in the cozy seating area. There were four men sitting at a table near the large bay window that overlooked the lake. All were dressed casually in ski attire, and unless she was mistaken, the youngest of the group was none other than world-class snowboarder Sean Wright.

On the opposite side of the room, a man sat on one of the overstuffed sofas that were strategically arranged around the huge fireplace. To his left, a tall woman dressed entirely in black peered out of a window overlooking the front drive. She appeared to be alone, and based on her position at the front of the room, Tj assumed she was waiting for someone to arrive.

"Is that Sean Wright?" Tj asked the resort's customer service manager, Leiani Pope, who had returned from upstairs just as Tj reached for the computer to confirm her suspicion.

"Yeah, he checked in this afternoon."

"Wow, he's even more of a babe than he appears in pictures." Tj couldn't help but admire the tall man with dark hair, blue eyes, and a huge smile.

"He seems really nice too. Not at all like the other one."
Tj knew Leiani was referring to Travis. "Isn't that Roger
Long sitting with Sean?"

"Yeah. I guess he's Sean's new coach."

Tj knew Roger Long had been the longtime coach of top-
ranked snowboarder Walter Tovar before he'd unexpectedly
retired the previous summer. Tj supposed Sean must have
hooked up with Roger at some point after that. Sean was
considered to be the second-ranked snowboarder now that
Walter had retired and Travis had moved up. Chances were,
Sean's association with the famous coach was making Travis
more than a little nervous.

"So why are Sean and his coach here in Serenity?"

"I talked to Coach Long for a few minutes when they
checked in," Leiani informed Tj. "He mentioned that Sean
hoped to use the carnival as a platform to gain recognition
among the larger international sponsors. Based on the
conversation we had, I'm guessing the other two men are
representatives from International Ski Corporation. I overheard
them talking, and it seems like they're considering sponsoring
Sean for the upcoming season."

Tj thought about Travis and the sponsorship he was
working to gain. She supposed obtaining big-dollar deals was a
competitive game that created a motivation above and beyond
the drive to win strictly for the sake of personal glory. For many
athletes, the wealth they accumulated as professional athletes
had a lot more to do with the symbols on their shirts than the
prize money from the competitions they won.

"And the ski bunny on steroids?" The woman Tj referred to
was short and thin with huge blond hair and an enormous chest,
which she'd encased in a tight red sweater atop body-hugging
black leggings. To top things off, she had on enough makeup to

appear clownish and was entertaining herself by reading Kierkegaard.

"She's not a guest," Leiani said. "I can ask her to leave if you want, but she isn't making any trouble."

"No, she's fine. I really should get going."

CHAPTER 6

Monday, February 17

Tj looked at the scoreboard and smiled. After a week of focused drills, her team looked better than ever. If they had a good showing during carnival, they might actually go into regionals with a lead. The competition slated for Thursday consisted of four men's events and four women's. The competitors were given individual scores and the teams were ranked based on the total number of points earned by the members of the group.

"Anyone seen Sarah and Eric?" Tj wondered. She hated to start her wrap-up until everyone was present.

"They had a fight and took off," Brittany shared.

"Dare I ask what the fight was about?" Tj had learned a long time ago that part of being a successful coach was to be a good mediator.

"Sarah's been hanging with Travis all week and Eric is jealous," Jilli informed her.

"Travis Davidson?" Tj asked. "Isn't he a little old for her?"

Jilli shrugged. "I guess. All I know is that Sarah ran into Travis while we were walking over from the locker room, and he invited her to go for a drink. She accepted and Eric went nuts. Sarah left with Travis and Eric stormed off in the opposite direction. I'm pretty sure Sarah is in the bar at the Inn, if you want me to get her."

"Thanks, but I'll stop by to check on her after we finish here. Chances are the bartender kicked her out anyway. She *is* only seventeen."

Jilli shrugged. "She got served last night. Guess Travis has enough clout that the guy looked the other way."

"Terrific." Not only was Tj worried that Sarah was much too young and inexperienced to take up with the likes of Travis Davidson, but she was equally concerned that a few illegal drinks could make the difference in her race times. "Okay, let's go ahead and get started. First of all, I'd like to congratulate each and every one of you on your effort today. You were all awesome. Connor and Brittany set personal bests, Jilli tore it up in spite of her knee, and Gary shaved enough time off of his runs to kick us up in the overall standings if he can duplicate the effort on Thursday.

"Tomorrow is our final practice before the qualifying heats scheduled for Wednesday," Tj continued. "We start off with the giant slalom, so I figured we'd focus on that tomorrow. I think with a strong showing we can edge into first place with overall points. The guys take the slopes first, but the girls will have their chance in the afternoon."

"I wish we were going earlier," Brittany complained. "I hate all the waiting around."

"Yeah, it sucks," Tj agreed. "But if we do well on Wednesday, we'll be seeded higher for the actual competition on Thursday. It's important that we stay focused. I want everyone to get a good night's sleep, and we'll meet back here after school tomorrow."

"I have a chem test to study for," Connor said. "I'll probably be up most of the night."

Tj frowned. School was closed for the winter carnival on Thursday and Friday, and Wednesday was a minimum day so Greg had excused the members of the downhill team because they'd be busy with qualifying heats. Her downhill team was expected to attend classes on Monday and Tuesday of carnival week, but Serenity was a ski town, and everyone knew how important it was to score well in the regional competition, so most teachers gave the kids a break and didn't assign important tests during those two days. The chemistry teacher was new to the area, so Tj gave him the benefit of the doubt.

"I'll talk to your teacher," Tj promised Connor. "He might not be aware of carnival-week protocol. If I can't get him to change the test date for everyone, I'll at least see if I can get him to let you take the exam next week."

"Thanks, Coach."

"Okay, I'll see you all tomorrow," Tj said, excusing her group.

The bar at the Angel Mountain Inn was packed. Tj waved to Albert Pitman, the Inn's owner, who was talking to Sean Wright. Sean was sitting at a table near the back, with his coach, Roger Long, Barney Johnson, and local downhill coach Steve Parker. Tj looked around the room until she spotted Sarah, who was sitting at a table with Travis and a couple of the girls from the Aspen Grove team. At least she appeared to be drinking soda. Tj was considering whether or not to head over and remind her that she'd missed the team meeting when Kyle walked in.

"Hey, Kyle. I didn't know you were here."

"I wasn't until just a little while ago. I wanted to come by to watch the kids practice. Everyone did really well, especially Connor."

"He did awesome, didn't he?"

"He really did. I couldn't be more proud if he were my own son."

"I'm afraid that's one of the benefits as well as one of the liabilities of working so closely with the kids. You form meaningful relationships that you cherish while they're with you, but then they graduate and move on. I've been doing this long enough that I'm pretty used to it, but I remember how devastated I was when my first group of seniors graduated."

"Yeah, I can see that. I've only been working with Connor for a little over a week and I already feel like a proud papa. I guess I never stopped to think about what it's going to be like when all these kids leave for college. Has Connor mentioned where he might be attending?"

"I think he's considering several..." Tj stopped talking in midsentence. She frowned as she looked toward a group of patrons sitting around the floor-to-ceiling fireplace.

"Something wrong?"

"See that woman sitting on the sofa reading?"

"The one dressed like Dolly Parton?"

"I keep seeing her at the resort, although she isn't a guest," Tj told Kyle. "The first time was on Friday. I've seen her twice since then, and each time she's wearing an outlandish outfit while sitting alone reading a book."

"And you find that...strange?"

"Yeah, I guess. It's not just that she's dressed like a ski bunny, it's that everything about her is so over the top. And every time I see her, she's alone and reading. Her behavior and outward appearance really don't match."

"Why don't you go talk to her to see what she's up to?"

"I would, but I'm actually here to check up on Sarah and probably shouldn't let myself get distracted." Tj looked back toward the table where Sarah sat with Travis. "She skipped out on the team meeting, and Jilli says she's been spending a lot of time with Travis. She's much too young to be hanging out with someone like that."

"Someone like what?"

"A player."

"I hear what you're saying and I don't disagree, but do you think embarrassing her in front of her crush will do any good? When you were her age, what would you have done if one of your teachers interfered with your date?"

"I probably would have told him to mind his own business. Of course, most of my teachers would have just gone straight to my dad, who would have killed me, effectively eliminating the middleman."

"I guess you could talk to Sarah's parents," Kyle suggested.

"Yeah, maybe. Her dad isn't in the picture, but her mom seems like an attentive if somewhat busy parent."

Tj watched as Chelsea Hanson stormed in through the front door of the bar. She looked around and then made a beeline toward Travis, who she soundly slapped before calling him every derogatory name in the book. Travis started to get up, but Chelsea slapped him again before leaning in and saying something Tj couldn't hear and then turning to leave the same way she'd come in. Travis said something to Sarah, got up, and followed Chelsea out.

"This might be your chance," Kyle whispered.

"Wait here."

Tj walked across the room and sat down in the chair Travis had just vacated. Sarah was in tears by this point, so Tj holstered the lecture she'd been prepared to deliver and hugged her instead. This wasn't the first time Tj had held one of her girls while she cried, and it wouldn't be the last. If there was one thing you could count on in life, it was the fact that teenage girls filled with teenage hormones were more often than not in a state of crisis.

After the other girls at the table left and Sarah finished crying, Tj handed her a napkin to wipe her face. "I missed you at the team meeting today."

"I know." Sarah hiccupped. "I'm sorry. I ran into Travis and he invited me for a drink. I thought we were going to talk about last night."

"Last night?"

Sarah blushed.

Oh. Suddenly, Tj realized how far Sarah's infatuation had gone.

"I thought he cared about me." Sarah started sobbing again. "He seemed so nice, and he really seemed interested in what I had to say. Everything was great until..." Sarah hesitated. "He wanted to...well, you know. I got scared, and things didn't go all that well. When I saw him today, I thought he wanted to apologize, but then his old girlfriend showed up, and suddenly he's dumping me to take off after her."

Tj sat quietly while she considered what to say. Part of her wanted to ask the poor girl how she could have been such an idiot. Not only was Travis six years older than her, but he had a reputation for being a player of the sleaziest kind. But one look at the emotional turmoil the poor girl was suffering was enough to convince her to take a different approach.

"How about we get out of here? My car is out front. I'll drive you home and we can talk on the way."

"No, that's okay. I have my mom's car. I'm sorry I skipped out on the meeting. Was Eric mad?"

"Eric wasn't there. It seems he took off after you when you left with Travis."

"I guess I really blew it. He's never going to speak to me again."

"Maybe, but maybe not. Eric cares for you. Maybe if you have an honest conversation with him, you can work it out."

"I doubt it. I...well, I did that thing with Travis, and Eric and I, well, we never...It was so stupid. I love Eric; he should have been my first, not stupid old Travis. What am I going to do?"

Tj wrapped her arms around Sarah in a long supportive hug. "I don't know, sweetie. Sometimes we close doors we never wanted to. We can work to open them again, but in the end we all have to live with the consequences of our choices."

"I guess."

"I'm supposed to meet my choir kids in a little over an hour. Will you be okay?"

"Yeah, I'll be fine. I'm going to get my stuff and go home."

Tj hugged Sarah one more time before standing up and heading back to where she'd left her backpack with Kyle.

"Did you hear about the explosion they had last night?" Kyle asked Tj when she returned.

"Explosion?"

"I was chatting with a guy I know who works in the administration building while you were gone, and he told me that someone left some of the dynamite they use for avalanche control in the storeroom behind the office and the whole thing blew up."

"Blew up? Was anyone hurt?"

"Two maintenance workers were injured in the explosion, but so far it looks like there wasn't any loss of life. The fire started about an hour before anyone had called it in. One of the maintenance workers was setting up tables in the lodge, and he's the one who saw smoke coming from the office and went to investigate. When he realized the building was on fire, he called another maintenance employee for help. They tried to use hoses to put out the flames while they waited for the fire department to arrive. It seems both men suffered from smoke inhalation, and one of them received some pretty bad burns when the building exploded. It's amazing they weren't both killed."

"I wonder how the fire started," Tj said.

"My friend said that they've been investigating it but so far they don't know."

Tj looked at the clock on the wall. "I guess we should get going if we don't want to be late for the dress rehearsal."

"Right behind you."

CHAPTER 7

Tuesday, February 18

Tj pulled into the parking area of Angel Mountain Ski Resort early the next morning. It was barely six thirty and the ski lifts wouldn't be open to the general public for hours, but as the ski coach at the local high school, she had a key to the locker rooms. Grabbing the equipment she planned to use during practice that day, she piled everything onto the cart she'd brought from Maggie's Hideaway and pushed it over the ice-covered walkway toward the well-lit building.

"Morning, Tj," William Bolton, Angel Mountain's vice president in charge of operations, greeted her. "You're here early today."

"I wanted to drop off this stuff before I headed to work," she explained. "I promised a couple of the kids a ride here, so I figured I wouldn't have room for their equipment as well as my own. You're here early yourself."

"Mayor Wallaby called me in a panic. I guess Travis was supposed to have dinner with the men interested in sponsoring him for the upcoming season, but he never showed."

"I haven't seen him since yesterday. I was in the bar to talk to one of my students, who had been invited for a drink by the 'hero' the mayor has been trotting around town. Apparently, Travis—who, by the way, is much too old for a seventeen-year-old girl—had been coming on to her. When I arrived, they were at a table with some other people. Chelsea Hanson came in, slapped him across the face, and then left. He followed her out the door, and that's the last I saw of the toad."

"I'm sure the guy will show up. By the way, I caught the tail end of your workout yesterday," Will said. "It looks like Connor Harrington is on fire this year."

"Yeah, he's really improved his time over last year. He's hoping for a scholarship and is working hard to make sure that happens."

"Has he applied for one of the Angel Mountain scholarships?" Will helped Tj maneuver her cart over the curb lining the parking lot. "It's a competitive process, but I think Connor has a good shot at it."

"I'll mention it to him, but he's really looking for something that will pay for his entire education. Still, I guess every little bit helps." Tj slipped her key into the lock and turned the handle. Pushing her cart, she made her way to the back of the room, where the larger lockers for season-pass holders and ski-team members were. Pausing near the bank of lockers reserved for her team, she frowned. There was something on the floor.

"That looks like—"

"Blood," Tj finished for him.

She followed what appeared to be a trail of blood toward the very back of the room. "I think whoever was injured left through this door."

"That's odd." Will frowned as Tj stood in front of the emergency exit. "The only way the door can be opened without sounding the alarm is if it's deactivated first. The only people with the code are security staff and resort management, all of whom would have been obligated to report an accident." He pulled up the incident reports on his cell phone and scanned the most recent entries. "I don't see anything in yesterday's reports."

"Maybe they were in a hurry," she suggested.

Tj opened the door after Will punched in the code, and they both stepped out into the alley at the back of the building, which accessed other buildings in the ski village as well. She was trying to imagine where an injured skier might have gone when she noticed a spot of blood on the snow about ten feet from the doorway. That spot led to another one that took her to the back door of the Inn.

"It looks like the injured party was a guest who returned to his or her room after the accident," Will said.

Tj frowned. "Yeah, looks like." She fought the feeling of déjà vu that suggested that the trail of blood was really something more. "Do you have a key to this door?"

"I have the master key to Angel Mountain," Will confirmed.

"Maybe we should follow the trail to the end to make certain someone isn't seriously injured," Tj suggested.

Will opened the door, which led into the administration office located at the back of the Inn. There was no one in the office; most staff didn't arrive until eight o'clock. The night desk clerk was watching a movie in the lobby and hadn't noticed the pair arrive. Tj saw a chair tucked into a corner of the room. It was covered with a blanket and didn't seem to be out of place, but a little voice in the back of her mind nudged her to check it out further. She lifted the blanket and realized that it was actually a wheelchair.

Will went into the lobby to question the desk clerk, while Tj followed the faint trail from the office to the service elevator, which could only be accessed by code. Tj turned to Will when he walked up behind her.

"The night clerk doesn't know anything about an accident," he confirmed. "He said he came on shift at ten o'clock and the evening was uneventful."

"Do you know the code to access this elevator?" Tj asked.

Will punched in a series of numbers.

The door slid open and they both stepped inside. Tj pushed the button for the third floor, where the guest rooms were located. The elevator floor appeared to be clear of blood, but the trail resumed in the hallway just outside the elevator door. It looked like someone had tried to clean up the blood but had missed a few drops. It most likely wouldn't even be noticeable if they hadn't been looking for it; the carpet in the hallway was a deep burgundy. They followed the blood trail to a room at the end of the hall.

"That's the Summit Suite," Will informed her.

"Travis Davidson's room," Tj remembered.

She knocked on the door, but there wasn't an answer.

"He's probably still sleeping," Will said. "It *is* early."

"Yeah, probably." Tj hesitated and then knocked again. When no one responded, she tried the handle, which easily gave way. "The door's open."

Tj stepped into the room, followed closely by Will.

The suite contained a sitting area as well as a separate bedroom. Tj noticed that the contents of the desk and dresser appeared to have been disturbed. The door to the bedroom was closed, but Tj spotted a drop of blood nearby. She knocked and waited. If Travis was passed out after a long night of partying, he was going to be mad as hell that Tj had awakened him at such an ungodly hour, but if he was injured, he might need their help.

Tj opened the door when he didn't answer. Someone was in the bed with the covers pulled up over his head.

"I'd better check on him," Will said. "Wait here."

Tj waited by the door as Will pulled back the covers. "You'd better call 911."

Tj sat in the restaurant with a cup of coffee as she waited to find out when she'd be released to go. It had been over three hours and she was getting restless. She'd called the school and explained the situation, and Greg had assured her that he'd find a sub for her classes. Kyle had offered to give the kids she was planning to transport a ride out to Angel Mountain, but she really wanted to be cleared to go by the time the team arrived for practice.

"Sorry about the wait." Roy Fisher, one of the Paradise County deputies assigned to the Serenity office, sat down at the table across from her. "I need to take a statement and then you'll be free to go."

"Where's Dylan?"

"He's busy talking to the medical examiner."

Tj couldn't help the look of disappointment that crossed her face.

"What now, your old buddy Roy isn't good enough for you?" he teased. Roy had gone to Serenity High School before graduating and getting a job with the Paradise County Sheriff's Department. Although he was a few years older than Tj, she'd always considered him a good friend.

"Sorry." Tj blushed. "You know I'm happy to answer any questions you have," she said, trying for a lighter tone.

"Can you describe exactly what occurred this morning?" Roy asked.

"Before or after I found Travis's body?" she asked.

"Both, actually. Start with your arrival at Angel Mountain and work your way forward from there."

Tj replayed her arrival, her meeting with Will, and her journey through the grounds to the locker room. She described their discovery of what appeared to be a trail of blood, and her movement through the alley and into the lodge, and then Will's discovery of Travis's dead body in his bed.

"How long had he been dead?" Tj wondered.

"We won't know until the autopsy is performed, but the medical examiner is estimating time of death to be somewhere between five and seven o'clock last night."

Tj frowned. The lifts were closed by then, but there were still quite a few people milling around at that point. Someone must have seen or heard something.

Roy continued, "Did you see Travis while you were here yesterday?"

"Yeah. He was in the bar, talking to some snowboarders."

"And what time was that?"

Tj thought back. "I guess around four thirty."

"Did you speak to him?"

"No." Tj hesitated. She trusted Roy, but she didn't want to inadvertently bring Sarah and her involvement with Travis into the investigation if she didn't need to. "Do you have any suspects?"

"Just one," Roy said.

"And who might that be?"

Roy hesitated. "I really shouldn't say."

"Come on, Roy. You know I won't blab. Besides, you owe me for making me sit here for half of the morning."

"I guess it couldn't hurt. I overheard Boggs mention a press conference later this afternoon anyway."

"Boggs is here?"

"Yeah, he's decided to handle the case personally."

"Ah." Paradise County encompassed all of the towns and

settlements around Paradise Lake. The main county offices, as well as the main jail, were located in the larger town of Indulgence, on the south shore. The sheriff's office located in Serenity was a satellite operation with three deputy sheriffs, a receptionist, and a single holding cell. Sheriff Boggs worked out of the larger office in Indulgence and rarely bothered himself with incidents taking place on the north shore.

"I guess I'm not surprised. The death of a high-profile athlete like Travis Davidson is bound to make the national news. So who's the suspect?" Tj asked again.

"Chelsea Hanson."

"Chelsea?" Tj was shocked.

"I'm afraid the evidence is stacking up against her," Roy admitted. "Boggs had someone pick her up over an hour ago."

"She's in jail?"

"'Fraid so. And it looks bad for her. Not only did several witnesses report that she'd argued with Travis yesterday afternoon, they found an ice ax with blood on it in the trunk of her car."

Tj took a deep breath. She remembered Chelsea coming into the bar and slapping Travis. It made sense that she'd want to get back at Travis for what he'd done to her, and Tj hadn't been alarmed or surprised at the outburst. She remembered Chelsea leaving the bar and Travis following her. She'd been busy comforting Sarah and hadn't given a second thought to what happened after that. She knew Chelsea had participated in a climbing demonstration that day, so it made sense that she had her ice ax in her possession. Still, murder? Slapping Travis seemed like a very Chelsea thing to do, but driving her ax into his chest? That seemed very unlikely.

"Chelsea couldn't have done this," Tj argued.

"I know that," Roy admitted. "I've known her my whole life.

She can be a prima donna at times, but she's no killer. Still, it looks bad."

"You aren't going to keep her in jail, are you?"

"If it were up to me, I wouldn't, but Boggs is in charge of the investigation, and he has a pretty tight rein on things. Tim," Roy said, referring to one of the other deputies at the Serenity branch of the Paradise County Sheriff's Department, "and I talked about it, and we doubt there's going to be much we can do to sway the investigation. Boggs has made up his mind that he has his killer and his high-profile case is all wrapped up. It seems like he couldn't be more pleased that Chelsea appears to be guilty. Talk about publicity. Imagine the headline: Heiress kills national snowboarding champion. It's golden."

"Even Boggs wouldn't arrest someone for publicity," Tj pointed out.

"If he had enough cause, you bet he would."

"Have you even considered other suspects?" Tj asked.

"Tim tried to talk to Boggs about other potential suspects, but he was pretty much shut down. Part of the problem we're having is that Chelsea admits to being present when Travis was stabbed but refuses to say who did it."

"What? Why would she do that?"

Roy shrugged. "I guess she's protecting someone. Tim and I were hoping you might nose around a bit and see what you can turn up."

"Why me? You're the cop."

"True, but you're the one who solved the Zachary Collins murder. You've proved that you have good instincts when it comes to tracking down clues and uncovering the truth. Boggs has us jumping through hoops. *His* hoops. We're under quite a bit of scrutiny, but you aren't. If you snoop around, Boggs doesn't ever need to know."

"What does Dylan say?" Tj wondered.

"I haven't been able to discuss the matter with him," Roy admitted. "As lead deputy of the Serenity office, he's been tied up, talking to Boggs and the medical examiner."

"Okay, then what do you *think* he'd say about my poking around in a police matter?"

"He'd tell you to stay out of it. He wouldn't want you to get hurt. I don't want you to get hurt either, but if I know Boggs, he's not going to go out of his way to prove Chelsea's innocence."

Tj glanced out the window. It was starting to snow. Her team would be here in a little over two hours. She wouldn't have time to look into anything then, let alone a murder, but maybe after she was done for the day.

"Okay, tell me what you know. I'm not sure what I can do, but I'm willing to listen to what you have to say and take it from there."

Roy sighed in relief. "Tim and I interviewed the Angel Mountain staff. Several of them reported that Travis was in the bar having a drink when Chelsea came in. She argued with him, slapped him, and then stormed out."

That tracked with what Tj had observed the previous day.

"Travis followed her out of the bar. We have at least one witness who said Chelsea headed for the locker room after she left the bar, and she admitted to as much. She told Boggs she intended to get her belongings and go home. Travis came in while she was gathering her stuff and they continued the argument they'd had in the bar."

Tj cringed. She could see why Boggs had picked her up.

"And then?"

"She said that while they were arguing, someone came in, picked up her ax, which was sitting near her locker, and stabbed Travis with it. As I mentioned before, she won't say who. All she'll say is that after Travis was stabbed, he started yelling and cussing. She was afraid he was going to become violent before he passed out on the floor. Chelsea figured he was drunk. She said she checked for a pulse, which was strong. After that she checked the stab wound, which was barely more than a scratch. She's insisting the wound couldn't have killed him. She was trying to decide what to do when she heard someone come in the front door. She knew how it looked, so she grabbed her stuff and left through the bathroom window."

"Do we know who came in?"

"We don't."

"Let me get this straight," Tj said, trying to wrap her head around the whole thing. "Chelsea and Travis are arguing and a third party she refuses to identify comes in and stabs Travis. He passes out, but, according to Chelsea, isn't seriously wounded. Someone comes in, at which point she leaves. There's a trail of blood from the locker room to the Inn, so we have to assume that someone used the wheelchair to move him. That someone has to be Angel Mountain staff because the alarm on the emergency exit was deactivated and the freight elevator, which requires a code, was accessed."

"Sounds about right."

"Can I talk to Chelsea?"

"'Fraid not. Boggs isn't allowing any visitors."

Later that afternoon, Tj was focusing all her attention on her team. She'd told Roy she'd do what she could to help free Chelsea, but she knew if she was going to ask her kids to give 100 percent, she needed to give them the same. "Okay, Gary, it's up to you. You need a time of 2:26:06. I need you to stay low and watch your edges."

"I got this, Coach."

"I know you do." Tj slapped him on the back.

Poor Gary. Normally, Eric would be making this particular run, but neither Eric nor Sarah had shown up today, so Gary had been recruited to fill in at the last minute. Tj wasn't surprised Sarah hadn't bothered to honor her commitment to the team. She'd shared a brief but intense relationship with Travis and was most likely devastated at the news of his death. But Eric? Eric couldn't care less about Travis. Tj figured he'd be in seventh heaven and ready to roll.

"The snow on the left side of the track looks iffy once you reach the halfway point," Tj informed him. "I need you to stay toward the center of the run. Stay focused and you'll do great."

Gary pulled on his goggles. "See you at the bottom."

Giving him one last thumbs up, Tj said a silent prayer as he made his way to the starting gate. Coaching, she'd realized some time ago, was one quarter skill building and three quarters cheerleading and confidence building. If her kids believed they could win, then more often than not they did. If they let the competition cower them, they usually lost.

CHAPTER 8

Rob's was a comfy pizza joint with vinyl booths, red-checkered tablecloths, team pictures on the walls, video games, and the best pizza west of the Rockies. As it was on any given day, the place was packed with friends and neighbors sharing a cheesy pie and a pitcher of beer. Tj waved to several people before sliding into a booth in the corner. Just off the beaten path, the restaurant catered to locals rather than tourists, as the establishments on the main drag were known to.

After she'd spoken with Roy earlier in the day, Tj had called Jenna and Kyle and asked them if they could meet with her after she finished downhill practice for the day. Dylan was tied up, and if she was even going to consider getting involved in an investigation she had no business going anywhere near, she'd need the help of her two best friends.

"So where do we start?" Jenna asked after the waitress walked away with their order.

"I'm not sure," Tj admitted. "Chelsea is obviously protecting someone. She's sitting in jail rather than telling Boggs who stabbed Travis, so it must be someone she cares about. Maybe we should start with a list of people with motives to kill Travis and *then* try to figure out who Chelsea might sacrifice herself to protect."

"Good idea." Jenna grabbed a pad of paper and a pen from

her purse and handed it to Kyle, who'd volunteered to be recorder. "We'll put everyone we can think of on the list and then sort the suspects based on the likelihood that Chelsea would sacrifice herself to protect them."

"Right off the top of my head, I think we can put Barney Johnson on the list." Tj explained to Kyle Johnson's devotion to helping Travis get a start on the professional circuit, and Travis's total disregard for his contribution once he'd made it big. "He has motive and has been very vocal about the fact that Travis shouldn't be allowed to participate in the winter carnival. I saw him at Angel Mountain the day of the murder, so I know he had opportunity. The only thing I'm not certain of is whether or not Chelsea would feel the need to protect him."

"And let's not forget Steve Parker," Jenna added. "He gave up a chance to work with Sean Wright in order to coach Travis, who then dumped him. I don't know that Chelsea is particularly close to the man, but I can understand how he might be motivated to do harm to someone who has seriously derailed his career."

"Coach Parker is still in town?" Kyle asked.

"Yeah. He runs the ski and snowboard clinic up at Angel Mountain," Tj explained. "He still works with some of the local talent, but Travis was his ticket to the big time. I'm sure there isn't a day that goes by that he doesn't find himself wishing he'd decided to dump Travis and get on board with Sean."

"Isn't Sean Wright the other snowboarder doing demonstrations this week?" Kyle wondered.

"Yeah," Tj answered. "He's worked himself into a solid second place in terms of national attention, behind Travis. He's staying at Angel Mountain, and I know he's been meeting with representatives from some pretty big companies."

"Which I guess gives him motive as well," Jenna said.

Kyle added him to the list. "Anyone else?" he asked.

"There are quite a few local businesses that threw money at Travis's career in the hopes of getting national exposure as a sponsor once he made it big," Tj added. "I don't know if any of the merchants affected by Travis's defection are mad enough to kill him, but we can keep the possibility in the back of our minds."

"Jeremy Young from Angel Mountain Sports and Pete Quinn from Quinn's Boards and Skis were the largest contributors to Travis's bank account," Jenna said. "I'm sure it stung when the guy dumped them without a how-do-you-do, although Pete at least appears to be doing well without Travis."

"Why do you say that?" Kyle asked.

"He just completed a major remodel on his store," Tj supplied. "It's absolutely gorgeous."

"Okay, are there any other local businessmen who might want to off the guy?" Kyle asked.

"There are a lot of local businesses that invested in Travis, but the list is pretty long and most sponsors were into the guy for a relatively minor amount," Tj said. "My dad gave Travis money, but there's no way I'm adding him to that list."

"Agreed," Kyle answered. "So who else *should* we add?"

"The guy has been making waves since he's been in town. I know Murphy was madder than hell when Travis started a fight that resulted in a significant amount of damage to his bar, and Albert Pitman complained that Travis was disturbing his other guests with his parade of women. And let's not forget about me," Tj added.

"You?" Jenna asked.

"Everyone knows I wanted to wring his neck for messing with my kids. My kids." Tj paled. "Oh God, I think I know who might have done it."

"Who?" Kyle and Jenna asked in unison.

Tj felt like she might cry.

"Are you okay?" Jenna put her arm around her.

Tj took a deep breath, then looked around the room to make sure no one was listening. "The entire time we've been making this list, I kept thinking that while each and every person on it had a motive, not one of them seemed like someone Chelsea would sacrifice herself to protect. And then I remembered Sarah."

"Sarah from the bar," Kyle realized.

"Sarah who from what bar?" Jenna asked.

Tj explained about the short-lived love affair between Travis and one of the girls on her downhill team. "Sarah thought he cared about her. She was devastated when she found out he didn't. Sarah was at the bar with Travis. Chelsea came in, said a few choice words, then stormed out. Travis followed her and I went to talk to Sarah. I was with her for a while, but I had to get going to be on time for the dress rehearsal. She was still at the bar when I left. What if she heard Chelsea and Travis fighting and went into the locker room? Maybe Chelsea's ice ax was sitting conveniently on a bench and she picked it up and stabbed the bastard who broke her heart? And Chelsea couldn't bear to turn her in, so they fled the scene of the crime?"

"I hate to say it," Jenna admitted, "but that theory makes more sense than any of the other suspects we've come up with so far. The question is, what should we do? If Chelsea wanted us to turn Sarah in to the cops, she would have talked to Dylan herself. There has to be another answer, another way to look at things."

"You make a good point," Tj said. "Maybe we should talk to Sarah ourselves and then take it from there."

* * *

Sarah Blakely lived with her widowed mother on the outskirts of town. Tj knew the family had struggled since Mr. Blakely's death, as evidenced by the number of times Sarah had had to miss class or downhill practice because she was needed at home to babysit her younger siblings. Kyle, Jenna, and Tj had discussed it, and they'd decided that Tj would go alone to talk to the girl. If she did kill Travis, she was most likely frightened, and a large group coming at her all at once might do more harm than good.

"Coach Jensen?" Sarah answered the door. Her face was pale and the swelling around her eyes made it appear that she hadn't stopped crying since the previous day. "I'm sorry I missed practice today. I had to stay home to watch my brother and sisters."

"Is your mom home?" Tj wasn't sure she should question a minor without her mother's presence.

"No, she's at work."

Tj could hear the sound of kids arguing over the cartoons playing in the background. She could leave and come back at another time, but if Sarah had killed Travis, the poor girl was probably stressed to the max. Leaving her alone with her brother and sisters when she might not be emotionally stable didn't seem like the right thing to do either.

"Would it be okay if we talked for a minute?"

Sarah looked nervously behind her. Tj could see that a boy who looked to be around ten and two little girls who seemed to be a couple of years younger were watching them from behind the couch. "Maybe we should talk outside," Sarah suggested. "Just give me a minute to get my coat."

"I'll wait here on the bench."

Tj sat down on a hardwood bench that was situated to the left of the front door on a covered front porch. A black cat sat in the living room window and a small tan and white dog peered at her from a doghouse on the edge of the enclosed porch. She prayed Sarah hadn't killed Travis, but deep in her gut she felt she most likely had.

"I think I know why you're here." Sarah sat down quietly next to Tj, who waited for her to continue. "I didn't mean to do it."

"Can you tell me what happened?" Tj placed her arm around the girl, who had begun to cry.

"I was a virgin, you know. Eric and I have been dating for a long time, but I told him I wanted to wait. I dated a few guys before Eric, and they broke up with me the minute I told them I wasn't ready. But Eric was different. He not only didn't break up with me, he didn't even get mad. When I told him that I wasn't ready to," Sarah hesitated, "become intimate, he looked me in the eye and told me he loved me. He told me he'd wait forever if need be."

Sarah started sobbing so hard, Tj was afraid she'd hyperventilate. Tj tightened her arms around the devastated teenager and held her until the tears lessened. Finally, after several minutes, she looked up and accepted the tissue Tj handed her.

"I really blew it," she continued. "I was so stupid. Eric loved me, and I threw it all away to pant after some jerk who could barely remember my name."

"Do you want to tell me what happened with Travis?" Tj asked gently.

"I was at the lodge after practice. I was supposed to meet up with Brittany and Jilli, but they were late. Travis walked in, and I recognized him immediately. He used to hang out with my older sister. She's in college now, but I used the connection to introduce myself. He was so nice and *so* charming. He said he remembered my sister, and he complimented me on what a 'babe' I'd grown into. He offered to buy me a drink. I know I'm too young to drink and should have said no, but I was flattered that this famous guy would be interested in me. I guess I sort of lost my head."

Tj sat quietly and waited for Sarah to go on. She'd learned a long time ago when speaking to her students about matters of the heart, it was usually best to let them set the pace.

"We hung out over the next few days. At first it was casual, but as time went by, things got a little more physical. When it came time to"—Sarah stopped speaking and looked at the ground—"well, you know, I sort of freaked. I mean, I'd never done it before, and it didn't feel right. I told him I didn't want to do it, but he called me a tease and he..." She started to cry again. "He forced me."

"Oh God," Tj breathed. "He raped you?"

Huge tears streamed down Sarah's face. "I don't know that rape is the right word. It started off as consensual, but when I got scared and told him I didn't want to go all the way, he called me a tease and made me finish anyway. The next day, when I saw him walking toward the bar, he apologized. He said he was drunk and didn't know what he was doing. Fool that I am, I believed him. He offered to buy me a drink so we could talk. I knew we had the team meeting, but it seemed so important, so I agreed."

"Then Chelsea came in," Tj supplied.

"Yeah. She was yelling and cussing, and I could tell she was mad as hell, but then I looked at his face. He was totally into her. She slapped him and left, and before I knew it, he'd left me sitting alone to go after her."

"And that's when I came over."

"Yeah."

"I'm so sorry I left you. I should have made sure you got home safely." Tj hugged the fragile girl.

"It's not your fault. I told you I'd go home, and I would have, but I remembered that I'd left my jacket in the locker room. I went back to get it, and Travis and Chelsea were in there fighting. She was accusing him of seducing another girl she knew. She said he'd ruined her life. He admitted it, and then the bastard started laughing like it was some big joke. I don't know what happened. I saw the ax sitting on the bench and I totally lost it. I picked it up," Sarah started sobbing again, "and stabbed him in his cheating heart."

"And Chelsea?" Tj asked after a few minutes.

"She told me to go home. She told me she'd take care of it. I came straight home and haven't left the house since. I didn't even know the guy was dead until an hour ago. I know I stabbed him, but he seemed mad rather than dead. He was yelling at me, and I thought he was going to hit me or something, but then he started to stumble around like he was totally tanked. He got this strange look on his face and fell on the floor."

"How'd you find out he was dead?" Tj wondered.

"Eric called. I told him everything."

"Is he the only other person who knows?"

Sarah's eyes filled with tears. "I guess. Unless Chelsea told someone."

Tj was trying to decide how to proceed when her phone rang. She looked at the caller ID. "Hey, Roy."

"I thought you should know that someone confessed to killing Travis."

"Really? Who?"

"He's a minor, so I can't divulge the name."

Eric. "I know this is going to sound ridiculous, but he didn't do it."

"How do you know? I haven't even told you who it is."

"I just know. Is Boggs still there?"

"No, he went back to the south shore for the day."

"How about Dylan?"

"Yeah, he's here."

"Have they released Chelsea?"

"No, not yet."

Tj hesitated. "Okay, I need to talk to someone. I'll call you back in a few minutes."

CHAPTER 9

After Tj explained everything to Sarah, she insisted on turning herself in. The last thing she wanted was for Eric to deal with the consequences of her behavior. Tj called Sarah's mother, who was understandably upset and came home immediately, and the three of them went to the sheriff's office together. Tj called Dylan prior to their arrival and briefly described what had happened.

"I didn't mean to kill him." Sarah sat with her face buried in her crossed arms, sobbing uncontrollably. "I was just so mad when I heard him laughing about molesting that other girl."

"You didn't kill him," Dylan assured her.

"I didn't?" Sarah looked up.

"The medical examiner determined that the injury inflicted by the ice ax was little more than a surface wound. It bled a lot but did no real damage. What happened after you stabbed him?"

Sarah stared at the white wall as she tried to organize her thoughts. "He was so mad," she said. "He was yelling and cussing, and I thought he was going to hit me." She took a deep breath before continuing. "But then he started stumbling around and fell to the ground. I thought he was dead, but Chelsea said he was just drunk. Her dad is a doctor, so I figured she knew what she was talking about."

"What happened after that?" Dylan handed Sarah a box of Kleenex.

"Chelsea told me to go home. She said she'd take care of it. I know I should have told someone, but I was confused and didn't know what to do."

"Is there anything else you can remember?" Dylan asked gently.

"No. I went straight home after Chelsea told me to leave. I didn't talk to anyone."

"Okay, I guess that should do it for now." Dylan closed his notebook.

"Are you going to arrest me?" Sarah looked as pale as a ghost.

"No, at least not at this time. I'll need to discuss the case with Sheriff Boggs. Right now, I'd like you to go home and stay there until I notify you. Don't leave your house and don't talk to anyone about this."

"Okay." Sarah was shaking as she tried to stand.

Dylan stood up to escort Sarah and her mother out of the office. He gently took Sarah's arm and helped to steady her on her feet. "You did the right thing coming in," Dylan assured her. "I can't say for sure what the sheriff will do, but I want you to know that I think you were brave to talk to me."

"Thanks." Sarah smiled through her tears.

Tj remained in Dylan's office after Sarah and her mother left. The fact that Travis hadn't actually died from the wound Sarah had inflicted reduced the possible charges against her from murder to assault. There was a good chance she'd get off with counseling and probation.

"So why is Chelsea still in custody?" Tj had to ask.

"She's still our number-one suspect," Dylan answered.

"But Sarah just confessed to stabbing Travis. Chelsea was just trying to protect her. Surely that's not a crime punishable by jail time."

"No, it isn't, but killing someone is. Travis didn't die from the wound to his chest," Dylan reminded her.

Tj frowned. "How did he die?"

"He was suffocated. It appears someone put something over his face and held it there until he was dead."

"And Sarah just testified that she left Travis alone with Chelsea, who said she'd take care of it," Tj said. "I know it seems like Chelsea must have suffocated Travis while he was passed out drunk, but I know her; she wouldn't have done that."

"Travis wasn't drunk," Dylan shared. "He was drugged by someone in the bar just prior to chasing after Chelsea."

Tj groaned. "You think Chelsea slipped something into his drink when she was at his table arguing with him?"

"It's a theory," Dylan admitted. "I'm not saying it's *my* theory, but at this point it's the one Boggs is going with."

"I need to talk to Chelsea."

"Sorry. Boggs is insisting that no one other than her attorney can talk to her."

Tj began pacing around the office, trying to figure out a way to help Chelsea. She'd done a brave thing by covering for Sarah and didn't deserve to spend another night in jail. Not that the little jail at the Serenity station was all that bad. Most inmates, once booked, were transported to the larger jail at the county office in Indulgence because the Serenity sheriff's office was so small. When she'd walked past the single cell with Sarah and her mother, Tj had noticed that someone, most likely Roy, had provided Chelsea with all the comforts of home, including a television and a home-cooked meal. Someone had even hung a blanket around the bed to afford her some degree of privacy.

"Okay." Tj stopped pacing and faced Dylan. "One theory is that Chelsea did kill Travis. He's been a thorn in her side all week, he assaulted poor innocent Sarah, and she finds herself alone with him in the locker room. He's passed out and unable to fight, so she grabs something handy, puts it over his face, and suffocates him." Tj took a deep breath. "A second, much better theory, in my mind, is that Chelsea left before Travis was suffocated. Chelsea admitted she was left with Travis, but then she heard someone come in. At that point she says she left by climbing out of a bathroom window. Maybe the person who came in moved Travis to his room and then suffocated him."

"Why would someone do that?" Dylan asked. "If someone wanted to kill Travis, why not leave him where he was?"

"I don't know," Tj admitted.

"It's late and I have a lot of paperwork to do if I'm going to get this wrapped up." Dylan put his hands on Tj's upper arms. "Go home and get some rest. I don't think Chelsea did this any more than you do, but I'll need some proof if I'm going to convince Boggs to let her go."

"She'll be okay?"

"Roy is treating her like the queen herself. She's not thrilled to be here, but she'll be fine."

Tj laid her head on Dylan's shoulder, drinking in his warmth, before stepping back. "I've missed you the past couple of days."

"I've missed you too."

"I guess you've been busy," Tj fished.

He nodded. "Not only are we still investigating the explosion at Angel Mountain, but now we have the murder of a high-profile snowboarder to deal with. Chances are I'll be here most of the night."

"See you tomorrow?" Tj asked hopefully.

"Most definitely."

After Tj left the sheriff's office, she called Jenna and Kyle. Luckily, Dennis was home and happy to watch Kristi and Kari, and her dad was likewise able to watch Ashley and Gracie. After the emotional rollercoaster of the past twelve hours, Tj needed a little best-friend time. The three friends agreed to meet at Murphy's Bar, a local favorite for the good food, reasonable prices, and friendly service.

"Hey, guys, what can I get yah?" Murphy, a first-generation Irish immigrant with a strong accent and an inviting smile, asked when Tj walked in with Kyle and Jenna.

"Just a cola for me," Kyle answered.

"Make that two," Tj added.

"Three," Jenna chimed in.

"Go ahead and get a table," Tj instructed. "I'll get the drinks."

Murphy's had been her grandfather's hangout since before Tj was born. Some of her earliest memories were of sitting next to her grandpa at the bar, sipping a soda and watching a game on television.

Technically, a five-year-old wasn't allowed to sit at a bar, even in the state of Nevada, but at Murphy's no one stood on formality and law enforcement most often turned a blind eye.

"I heard they arrested Chelsea Hanson for killing Travis Davidson," Murphy commented as he set three frosty glasses on the bar.

"Afraid so," Tj said.

"Heard you might be looking into things."

Tj frowned. "Who told you that?"

"A little bird." Murphy was a short and slightly plump man in his mid-sixties who had his ear to the ground and knew everything that was happening in town at any given time.

"I told a friend I'd keep my ears open, but I'm not a cop, so officially I'm not investigating anything."

"Well then, unofficially, I might have a different suspect for you," Murphy informed her.

"Really? Who?"

Murphy leaned in close and whispered, "Josh Steinbeck."

"What?" Tj coughed on the sip of soda she'd just taken. "Why in the world would you think Josh killed Travis?" Josh Steinbeck was Dennis's engine partner and best friend.

"Guess you heard about the explosion up at Angel Mountain," Murphy continued in a quiet voice, even though there was so much noise in the room that no one could have overheard them even if they were speaking in a normal tone.

"So?"

"Did you know that two maintenance workers were injured in the fire?"

"Yeah, I heard something about that," Tj confirmed.

"One of the men received third-degree burns. They had to airlift him to Sacramento for treatment. The man—who, by the way, might lose his arm—is Josh Steinbeck's father, Bert Sanders."

Tj frowned. "Is he going to be okay?"

"Too early to tell." Murphy shook his head.

"I'm surprised Jenna didn't mention anything to me."

Murphy shrugged. "Doubt she knows. Josh's parents were divorced a long time ago."

"If you don't mind my asking, how do you know all of this?"

"A few years ago, Bert came back onto the scene. Bert and Josh have been working on developing some sort of relationship, but they've been keeping it quiet so as not to upset Josh's mom. The only reason I know about the connection is because Bert comes into the bar every now and then, and he starts to ramble after a few drinks. Based on what he's told me, Josh wanted nothing to do with him when he first came back to town, but in recent months he's felt like Josh has opened up to the possibility of a relationship."

"As interesting as this information is, I don't see how that would make Josh a suspect in Travis Davidson's murder," Tj pointed out.

"Josh was in the bar having a cold one two nights ago," Murphy went on at his own speed. "I overheard him talking to someone on the phone. When he finished with his call, I could tell he was madder than a cat on a hot tin roof. I managed to get him talking, and he told me that the fire at the resort wasn't an accident. Someone intentionally set it and, according to Josh, the person who did it was Travis Davidson."

Tj frowned. "Why would Travis burn down the administration building?"

"That I don't know." Murphy wiped down the bar with a damp rag. "What I do know is that Josh was about as mad as I've ever seen a man. He slammed out of here promising revenge."

"Thanks for the info." Tj picked up the drinks. "Promise me you won't share this with anyone else until I figure out what to do with it?"

"Don't worry. I can keep my mouth shut," Murphy assured her.

Tj doubted it, but she supposed she didn't have much control over the situation.

"What gives?" Jenna asked as soon as Tj returned to their table. "You look like you've seen a ghost."

Tj filled them in on her conversation with Murphy. With Boggs involved in the investigation, there was no way she was going to tell Dylan or anyone else who might be obligated to report what Murphy had told her to the sheriff. She'd talk to Josh herself and then decide what to do.

"There's no way Josh would kill anyone," Jenna insisted. "I'm sure he must have confided in Dennis. They *are* best friends. I'll call him and see what he knows."

Tj watched Jenna's face lose color as she talked to her husband. She couldn't hear Dennis's end of the conversation, but she was willing to bet it wasn't going well.

"What is it?" Tj asked as soon as Jenna hung up.

"Josh has been off shift, the same as Dennis, since the fire, but he's supposed to work tomorrow. He called in a little while ago and requested time off. I asked Dennis if he'd spoken to him since Sunday, and he said he'd left a bunch of messages for him, but he hasn't returned any. You don't think...?"

Tj didn't think Josh was capable of killing Travis, but Boggs would jump all over this if he found out about it. Tj didn't know who had called Josh or where he'd gone, but she knew she couldn't go to the authorities yet, so it was going to be up to her to find out.

CHAPTER 10

The trio decided to move the conversation over to Jenna's house so Dennis could participate. The Elstons lived on the outskirts of town in a large two-story house situated on ten acres of pristine forest bordering the Paradise River. Although it was late and Tj longed to go home and climb into her big bed, she knew she owed it to everyone involved to help figure out what, if anything, they could do to help Josh before Boggs found out about his outburst in the bar and issued an APB for his arrest.

"There's no way Josh killed anyone," Dennis insisted. Kristi and Kari were long asleep, so they had to keep their voices down as they sat around the kitchen table. "I've left ten more messages since you called, but he isn't picking up his cell."

"You know him better than anyone. If he was upset and wanted to disappear, where would he go?" Tj asked.

Dennis thought about it. "He likes to go fishing along the American River, but given that it's two degrees outside, I doubt that's where he went. His uncle has a cabin up north that he talks about now and then, but I'm not sure exactly where it is. I suppose his mom would know. I could give her a call, but she'd wonder why I was asking, and I hate to upset her if I don't need to."

"What about his friend in Pismo Beach?" Jenna suggested. "He might be hiding out with him."

"I guess I could call him to see if he's heard from Josh."

"Maybe we're going about this all wrong," Kyle said. "We all believe Josh didn't kill Travis, and yet this entire conversation is based on the assumption that he *did* and is hiding out."

"Good point," Dennis acknowledged.

"Jenna mentioned you and Josh were supposed to work tomorrow, but that he called in and asked for time off," Kyle continued. "It seems to me that if Josh killed Travis and was on the run, he wouldn't take the time to call in to the station."

"So if he's not hiding out, where is he?" Dennis asked.

"Here's what I don't get." Jenna set a plate of homemade coffee cake on the table. If there was one thing you could say about Jenna, it was that she was the perfect hostess, no matter what the occasion. "The fire occurred on Sunday. Today is Tuesday. Murphy told Tj that Josh received a call on Sunday evening while he was in the bar. How come Josh knew that Travis was a suspect but Dennis hadn't heard? When Tj mentioned that Josh received a call, I assumed it came from Captain Brown, or maybe the investigator on the case."

"That's a good point." Dennis sat forward. "I've been off duty since the fire, and so has Josh. Why would someone call him and not me?"

"Unless they had a specific reason for calling Josh," Tj theorized. "In any other case, if you were off duty and information came forth about a case you weren't specifically working on, would you be called at home with an update?"

"No. Not unless they needed information from me, or the case was directly related to me in some way," Dennis confirmed. "It actually makes sense that no one called me. What doesn't make sense is that someone called Josh. We were both off on Sunday and only responded as backup support. We were the first engine to leave and were in no way involved in the investigation."

"Unless whoever called Josh knew that the man who was burned is his father," Jenna pointed out.

"Yeah, but supposedly no one knows that. Not even me, and I'm his best friend. When Bert Sanders was pulled out of the building and loaded onto the ambulance, Josh didn't say a word. He just focused on putting out the fire, gave me a high five when we were finally released to leave, and said he'd see me on Wednesday. I know what Murphy said about Bert being his dad, but even with that knowledge, I'm having a hard time believing it's true." Dennis rested his elbows on the table and put his head in his hands. "You'd think the guy would have said something, or at least have shown some sign of recognition."

"Don't feel bad, honey." Jenna put her arm around her husband. "Josh obviously is very motivated to keep his dad's identity a secret. I'm sure he would have told you eventually."

Dennis took a deep breath. "Yeah, I guess."

"Is there any way to find out who might have called Josh?" Tj asked.

"If it was an official call from someone at the station, I can probably find out who made it," Dennis said.

"How long would it normally take for the investigators to determine the cause of the fire?" Tj asked.

"Depends. In order to investigate, they need to wait until the structure cools down. The amount of time that takes depends on the severity of the fire, the air temperature, and whether or not an accelerant was used, among other things."

"Does it seem reasonable that a fire that completely destroyed a structure on Sunday evening would have cooled down enough for an investigation to be conducted later that evening?"

"No." Dennis looked up. "I see where you're going with this. In order for the call Josh received to have been official, an investigation would have had to have been completed. There's no way."

Tj looked out of the window at the snow that was starting to fall. She really should be getting home, but she didn't want to leave until they got this figured out. She supposed if the weather got too bad, she could spend the night and then get up early to go home to shower before she had to leave for work.

"We need to find out who called Josh," Jenna said.

"Dylan could get his phone records," Tj suggested.

"We can't tell Dylan until we clear Josh." Jenna looked concerned.

"I can get it," Kyle volunteered. Kyle was a computer genius who wrote software prior to moving to Serenity. If there was a database to hack into, Kyle was the man to do it.

Forty minutes later, Kyle had the number. It turned out that the cell phone used to call Josh belonged to Travis Davidson.

CHAPTER 11

Wednesday, February 19

For the first time in at least a month, Tj felt herself truly begin to relax. After weeks of hard work and a breakneck schedule, things were beginning to come together. Not only had her downhill team nailed the qualifying rounds they'd had that morning, but her choir had rocked the house during the opening ceremonies of the winter carnival. It would have been a perfect start to the day, except for the fact that they hadn't heard from Josh, Chelsea was still in jail, and Travis's killer had yet to be identified. Jenna reported that no one from the firehouse had heard from Josh, but the investigator's report supported that the fire had been arson. Apparently, Travis must have told Josh he set the fire, but that news wasn't widely known; the official report didn't list him as a suspect.

After the concert, Tj invited Jenna and Kyle to have a celebratory drink at the Beef and Brew, an upscale steakhouse situated right on the lake on the east end of town. During the summer, people came from miles around to dine on the deck overlooking the water, where large fire pits were placed strategically to give off cozy heat even on the crispest mountain evenings. And in the winter, diners could enjoy the view from the interior of the log building. Several real wood fireplaces provided enough warmth to keep things comfortable on the coldest days. The bar, where Tj and the gang decided to procure a table, was on the opposite side of the kitchen, as far away from the formal dining area as the building would allow. While the bar served good but simple fare such as wraps, pizza, sandwiches, and burgers, the dining room was famous for its intimate atmosphere, as well as steaks that literally melted in your mouth.

"To Kyle." Tj raised her glass. "For working a miracle and pulling together the best concert this town has witnessed in a very long time."

"Hear, hear," Jenna rang in.

Kyle blushed. "It was nothing. They're good kids who just needed a little direction. You have a lot of potential in that group. Even Marley wasn't too bad once I got her singing in the right key."

"Did I hear an offer to continue working as unofficial co-choir director?" Tj persuaded. "It's an unpaid position, but I don't suppose that matters much from where you're sitting."

"I'd love to continue on. I can't remember the last time I had this much fun. Although I'm not sure I can take much more of Marley's help as an assistant. I know this sounds ridiculous, but I think she has a crush on me."

Tj laughed. "And you're just figuring that out? The girl has been seriously crushing since the first time you walked in the door. I thought you knew."

"I'm afraid I missed that completely. I really think it'd be best if we spent less time together, but she's been a real trouper, so I'd like to let her down gently."

"No worries," Tj replied. Kyle was sweet to be concerned about Marley's schoolgirl crush. "I'll just tell her she's too valuable on stage and we can't waste her time with such menial chores. She's a diva by nature, so I'm betting she'll leap right onto that wagon."

"Thanks."

"No, thank *you*. I don't know what the choir would have done without you. You even got Kendall Grant to sing loud enough to be heard. She's so quiet in class that half the time I forget she's even there."

"Kendall is just shy, and fading into the background is the way she deals with it," Kyle informed her. "After I heard her voice, I knew she had potential, so I helped her to forget about the audience and look only at me. I told her she needed to sing loud enough so that I could hear her, and then I just kept moving farther away."

"Careful or she's going to be the next one crushing on her amazing director," Jenna warned.

"You think so?" Kyle looked genuinely concerned.

"Sure, why not?" Jenna answered. "You're young, good-looking, kind, and attentive."

"Sounds like someone else is crushing," Tj teased.

Jenna laughed just as Ben came in, with Doc and Bookman trailing behind him. "Congratulations," he said, hugging Tj. "Your group was fantastic."

"Thanks, Grandpa." Tj hugged each of the men in turn. "So what are you rabble-rousers up to?"

"Meeting Helen and Bonnie for a cold one. They should be here any time now."

"I thought Mom and Bonnie were watching the girls," Jenna said.

"They were, but Mike and Rosalie decided to take them

sledding after the concert. They're going to meet us later at the judging for the snowman contest."

"The table next to us is free. We can push them together if you want to join us," Tj offered.

"Sounds good," Ben answered just as Helen and Bonnie walked through the front door.

"How goes the investigation?" Bookman asked.

Tj filled him in on the latest developments, including Josh's disappearance after receiving a phone call from Travis on Sunday evening. "We all know that Josh could never have killed anyone, but I have to admit it has us worried that he left in a rage after talking to Travis and hasn't been heard from since. You hear about people who would never otherwise hurt anyone suddenly killing someone in a fit of rage."

"I wouldn't worry." Bookman placed his hand on Tj's shoulder in a gesture of comfort. "You said Josh took off on Sunday evening, but Travis wasn't killed until Monday night. If Josh was going to kill Travis in a fit of rage, he would have done so immediately. I really doubt the two are related."

"Good point."

"I talked to the coroner," Doc added. "It appears Travis was smothered quite a while after he passed out from a drug cocktail: at least an hour. In my opinion, that negates the theory that Chelsea smothered Travis after Sarah left, but Boggs isn't budging on his idea that she's the guilty party."

"I don't suppose Boggs would let you look at the body?" Doc had helped Tj out when Zachary Collins was murdered, and she knew he was much more skilled than the local coroner, in spite of the fact that he'd been retired for quite a few years.

"I already did," Doc confirmed. "Bruising under the arms and on one leg suggest that Travis was alive when he was moved to his room. Based on the TOD and the timeline relating to the events in the locker room, it's my opinion that Travis was drugged and then stabbed, and then he passed out, was moved to his room, and later was smothered."

"Chelsea wouldn't have had access to his room," Tj pointed out. "I can't believe Boggs is still holding her."

"I spoke to Boggs, who insists that Chelsea could have taken Travis's key when he was passed out and returned later to finish the job."

"That's ridiculous," Tj insisted.

"I have to agree," Doc concurred. "Still, the scenario is not impossible. I think Boggs will let her go after he has time to think about it."

"This whole thing is so frustrating," Tj vented. "What we need is another viable suspect. If we can't prove Chelsea didn't do it, we need to prove that someone else did. I have a busy week, but I'm going to talk to a few people to see what I can dig up. There seems to be a lot going on here, and it only makes sense that everything is related in one way or another. We just need to figure out how."

"Or not," Bookman commented. "I wrote a story once where there were a lot of events that seemed to go together but ended up not being linked at all."

"Terrific," Tj groaned.

CHAPTER 12

The park at the edge of town was lit up like a Christmas tree when hundreds of residents and visitors gathered for the annual snowman judging. There were five categories: most lifelike, funniest, scariest, most original, and best overall.

"How come they don't have those fire pits over here?" Gracie wondered as they walked toward their snowman. Metal trash cans with roaring fires had been placed strategically between larger fires built in pits.

"'Cause the snowmen would melt," big sister Ashley pointed out.

"But it's cold," Gracie whined. Her long brown ringlets were covered by a bright red cap that matched her down jacket.

"It looks like you got wet while you were sledding. As soon as the judging is over, we'll go inside where it's warmer."

"Here we are." Ashley stopped at a large group of snow figures. There were eight in all, five people descending in size, a dog, and two cats.

"We made the whole family." Gracie's huge brown eyes danced with excitement.

The first snowman in the group was tall and thin and wore one of her grandfather's old hats. The next was slightly shorter and just a tad stouter and wore her dad's forest-green scarf. The third was actually a snowwoman and wore the knit cap Tj had just bought a few weeks earlier. Next to the Tj figure was a slightly shorter snow girl with a pair of glasses, followed by a much shorter figure wearing Gracie's bunny mittens. Positioned in front of the snow people was a snow dog, made to resemble Echo, a pudgy cat she assumed was Cuervo, and a smaller cat she'd bet was supposed to be Gracie's cat, Crissy.

"Wow! How'd you get all of this done in one morning? Grandpa must have had a lot of energy today."

Gracie laughed. "Grandpa didn't help us at all."

"Yeah, he just sat over there on that bench with Doc and Bookman and made suggestions," Ashley added.

"Then how did you manage to do all this?" Tj was fairly certain one eight- and one five-year-old couldn't accomplish such a feat on their own.

"Uncle Kyle helped us before he had to leave for the concert," Gracie admitted.

"That was nice of him."

"Is Uncle Kyle our real uncle?"

"Of course not. What a dummy," Ashley teased.

"I'm not a dummy."

"Are so."

"We don't call people dummies," Tj reminded Ashley. "Now apologize."

"Sorry," Ashley offered reluctantly.

"So is he?" Gracie asked again.

"No, Kyle isn't your real uncle," Tj told her. "Real uncles are related to you by blood. Uncle Kyle is more of an honorary uncle."

"What's an honorary uncle?"

"It's a friend who cares about you and likes to spend time with you," Tj explained.

"Like Aunt Jenna and Uncle Dennis?" Gracie clarified.

"Exactly."

Gracie paused to consider this while Tj examined the snow family. "Why did you put glasses on the Ashley snow girl?" Tj asked.

Ashley shrugged. "Glasses are cool. I wish I could get some."

"Glasses are for people who need help seeing things either close up or far away. Your eyes are perfect," Tj pointed out.

"Glasses make you look smart. I'm tired of people treating me like a kid."

Tj wanted to point out that at eight she *was* a kid, but she knew her super-smart, mature-beyond-her-years sister wouldn't appreciate the reminder. "I don't recognize those. Where did you get them?"

"Deputy Dylan let me use them. I guess someone left them in lost and found a long time ago."

"Dylan was here?" Tj asked.

"Yeah, he helped us with the snow family. He gave us the collar we put on Echo and the string we wrapped around Crissy."

"That was nice of him."

"Grandpa says he's good folk," Ashley pointed out.

Tj knew her sister was right. Dylan *was* good folk.

"Is Grandpa really our grandpa?" Gracie was obviously still pondering the concept of real versus honorary family.

"No," Tj answered. "But he loves you like a real great-grandpa, just like Papa loves you like a real grandpa."

"Do we have any family that *is* real?" Gracie frowned.

"I'm your real sister," Tj offered as she knelt down and wrapped her scarf more snugly around her sister's neck.

The first-grader smiled. "I'm glad."

"Me too." Tj hugged her.

"So if you're our real sister and Papa is your real dad, how come we aren't really related to Papa?" Ashley joined the conversation.

"Well," Tj tried to decide how to best explain this, "once upon a time, our mom was married to Papa and they had me. Then they got divorced, and our mom married Jonathan, and they had you and Gracie. We have the same mom but different dads."

Ashley frowned but didn't say anything more.

"Do you think we're going to win?" Gracie asked, bringing things back around to the snow family.

"You never know what the judges are going to do, but I absolutely think you should," Tj responded.

"Uncle Dennis helped Kristi and Kari make a fireman snowman," Ashley informed her. "It's pretty good, but not as good as ours. Still, I think it should get a ribbon."

Tj looked to where Dennis, Jenna, Kristi, and Kari were standing in front of a life-size snowman dressed like a fireman. It was a bit more professional than the snow people Ashley and Gracie had built, but she hoped her sisters would get a ribbon in one of the categories. Whatever happened, Tj already felt like a winner. It had been a difficult six months since their mother's death, and she was glad to see that the girls were beginning to identify with their new family.

"Can we sit with Kristi at the spaghetti dinner?" Ashley asked.

"If we can find a table large enough for everyone." Tj waved at Jenna, who was holding four-year-old Kari.

"Here comes Uncle Kyle." Gracie pointed across the park.

Tj noticed Hunter leaving the sheriff's office which was just across the way.

"Listen, do you mind taking the girls inside?" Tj asked Kyle when he caught up with them. "I'll be there in a few minutes, but I want to say hi to Hunter. This whole thing has to be hard on him."

"Certainly. Take your time. I'll help the girls get their food."

"Thanks. I won't be long."

Tj had no idea what she was going to say to the man who had been such an important part of her life for such a long time. *Sorry to hear about your sister* seemed inadequate. In the end, she decided the most comforting words weren't words at all. Opening her arms as she walked toward him, he approached her and wrapped her in a body-engulfing hug that seemed to go on for a lifetime but probably actually lasted less than a minute. The sound of the carnival in the background seemed to exist in another realm as the tension in Hunter's body seemed to evaporate.

"I'm so sorry," Tj finally said. "How is she?"

Hunter pulled back just a bit. He looked deeply into her eyes, as if trying to memorize every feature. "I don't know." He released her, taking a single step back. "She's scared and confused. At first she was just protecting Sarah, and she figured everything would work out, but now that she realizes she was the last one to see Travis alive, she's really worried."

Tj threaded her fingers through his. "Let's take a walk."

"Yeah, okay," he responded tiredly.

They walked along the snow-covered beach hand in hand, each lost in their own thoughts. Tj couldn't imagine how hard this must be for him. He had always been the serious sort who tended to carry the cares of the world on his shoulders. It must be killing him that Chelsea was sitting in jail and there was nothing he could do to help her. Tj paused and looked out on the serene lake. It was one of those crisp but windless nights that created the illusion that the water was actually a sheet of glass.

"Is there anything I can do?" Tj asked.

"No." Hunter's breath hung on the cold air. "Our attorney says Chelsea swears she's innocent. According to her testimony, after Sarah left, she did a quick exam to make sure Travis wasn't actually in a life-threatening situation. She verified that the wound was little more than a scratch, and that his pulse and breathing were strong and steady. She figured he was drunk and would wake up with a hell of a hangover. She heard someone come in through the front door, so she went into the ladies' room and left thorough a window. She insists that she never wanted Travis to end up dead. She hoped the incident would serve as a wake-up call for him. I guess Sarah isn't the first minor Travis has seduced and then tossed aside. Chelsea told me he ruined the other girl's life, and she hated to see the pattern repeat itself with Sarah. When the sheriff told her that Travis was dead and took her in for questioning, she was shocked. She didn't want to implicate Sarah, so she decided to keep quiet until she could figure out how to handle things." Hunter turned and looked back toward the crowd lining the highway. "I suppose in the long run that was a huge mistake. Boggs doesn't trust her."

"I was just on my way to the spaghetti feed when I saw you come out of the county offices. Kyle and the girls are waiting for me, so I should get a move on. You can join us, if you want."

"Thanks, but I should be getting home. I hate to leave Grandfather alone for too long. We'll talk tomorrow."

"I'll call you." Tj tried to smile, but she knew the effort didn't reach her eyes.

Hunter kissed her lightly on the cheek. "Thanks, Tj. You're one of the few people in my life I know I can always count on."

Ben volunteered to take the girls home so Tj could visit some of the other venues with Kyle, who had shown up at the snowman competition in time to see the girls receive the ribbon for most lifelike. The Elston family's fireman snowman won best overall. It was a beautiful night. The fresh snow reflected the light from the almost full moon, creating a brightness that made navigating the narrow streets easier than it otherwise would have. The slight breeze that had given a chill to the air had stilled, causing the lake to appear as a glassy reflection of the scenery around it. While many of the family-oriented shops had closed, bars and restaurants were brightly lit, inviting in the casual passerby. Metal barrels containing wood fires had been distributed along the main drag, attracting groups of people who shared their warmth and caught up on the events of the day.

"It's really beautiful out here," Kyle commented. "When you mentioned a walk, I thought you were crazy, but it isn't cold at all."

"I'm sure the stocking cap, down coat, and leather gloves you have on help, but yeah, it's a beautiful night. Grandpa has the girls, so I thought we could wander around and check out some of the other venues."

"So what are our options?"

"The gymnasium at the high school will be open until nine. The home-crafted items that were judged today will be on display. I'm pretty sure Bonnie entered a quilt, and Jenna was planning to enter several baking categories. I forgot to ask how everyone did today, but whatever the outcome, I suppose that's an option."

"Sounds fun."

"The senior center is sponsoring ballroom dancing for all ages. I don't know about you, but I'm not really much of a dancer."

"Sounds like a pass," Kyle agreed.

"There's a music event known as Snowrama down by the beach. Basically, bands play a variety of music, with a giant bonfire and plenty of alcohol keeping everyone warm."

"So far I'm thinking that gets my vote."

"Yeah." Tj grabbed Kyle's hand. "Let's go."

"This is crazy," Kyle shouted over the sound of the music once they'd arrived. "Who would think to have an outdoor concert in February?"

"I know you'd think it would be unbearably cold, but between the bodies and the bonfire, it's actually quite pleasant."

Tj grabbed Kyle's hand as they inched their way toward the front. "By the way, thanks for helping the girls with their snowmen. Eight snow figures must have been a lot of work."

"It was fun. Those are some pretty great sisters you have."

"Do you have any siblings?" Tj wondered.

"No it's just Mom and me now that Dad has passed."

"You mentioned your mom was thinking about moving out to be near you?"

"Yeah. In a couple of months, I hope. It's been tough for her since my dad died. She has friends at home, but I think she wants to be close to the only family she has left."

"Is she going to move into the mansion with you? You have plenty of room." Kyle had inherited the Collins mansion on Heavenly Bay after Tj's friend Zachary had been murdered the previous fall.

"No. As much as I love my mom, I think we both need our own space. I was thinking about checking into the condos on Pine for her. They're close to town and have a view of the lake. Your grandpa told me the homeowners' association is very active. The complex is well maintained, and there are always a lot of planned activities for the residents."

"One of the teachers at the high school lives there. She really likes it. And Grandpa was right about the activities. They hold a buffet dinner for all the residents every Thursday, and the residents at the complex frequently organize wine tastings or sailing tours and invite everyone else."

"Sounds perfect."

"Hey, look, there's Connor and a couple of the guys." Tj waved to where Connor was talking with several other members of the downhill team. He broke away and headed toward them when he saw them.

"Hey, Coach, Kyle. Enjoying the tunes?"

"Yeah, they're really good," Tj agreed. "Are you out celebrating your victory this morning?"

"Totally. Not only did we steal the lead from Beaver Creek but Sean Wright came up to me after the competition and congratulated me. He said he might be interested in mentoring me if I was interested in going pro."

"Wow, that's quite an opportunity," Tj responded.

"I was really stoked when he first made the offer, but as much as I love to board, what I really want to do is help people. I'm thinking about trying out pre-med when I get to college. If I can get through the science *and* I can scrape together enough money through student loans and part-time jobs, I think I might want to be a doctor."

"You'd be a great doctor," Tj encouraged him.

"I think so too. My mom is worried about the cost of all the education though. She wants me to go to a trade school and major in something that will earn an income right away. My uncle is a mechanic, so I could always get a job in his shop. I enjoy working on my own piece-of-junk ride, but I don't know if

I'd want to do that as a career. I know that people sometimes have to settle, but I always dreamed of doing something more."

"Have you looked into private scholarships?" Kyle asked.

"Private? No. Mrs. Remington thinks I can qualify for some money through government-aid programs, and I've applied for an athletic scholarship that would help me out with the first four years if I stay healthy, but she hasn't mentioned private funding. Is that even a possibility?"

"Absolutely. Come to talk to me next week and we'll see what we can work out."

"Cool. Thanks, man." Connor looked toward his teammates. "I really should get back. See you tomorrow."

"You're going to pay for his college?" Tj asked as Connor walked away.

Kyle shrugged. "Zachary left me more money than I know what to do with. I've been thinking about putting aside part of it to set up a charitable foundation. Helping Connor seems like a good place to start."

Tj hugged Kyle. "You're a good guy. Zachary couldn't have left his money to a better person."

Kyle blushed.

"Oh look, there's Jeremy Young." Tj pointed across the mob of bodies dancing to the tunes. "Save my place and I'll see if I can get his alibi. He's not high on our list, but we need to start eliminating people."

Tj wormed her way through the crowd. It never ceased to amaze her how many people could mash into a small space. Normally, the proximity of so many people at one time would bring on feelings of claustrophobia, but tonight she was on a mission, her mind on little else.

"Hey, Jeremy," Tj greeted him. "Quite a crowd."

"Yeah, it's nuts here, but the music is the bomb."

"So I guess you've been busy this week," Tj fished.

"Slammed," he verified. "In fact, this is the first time I've been able to get down off the mountain before midnight all week."

"Wow, midnight. That's late. I thought you closed at seven."

"We do, but we got in a shipment of new boards on Monday and have been busy getting them all inventoried and prepped for sale."

"So you were around on Monday night?"

"Yeah. Why?"

"Just wondering if you were in a position to notice anything going on that might help us to identify Travis Davidson's murderer."

"Sorry, I never left the village. I heard they arrested Chelsea Hanson."

"Yeah. I'm trying to figure out how to get her off the hook."

Jeremy thought about it. "There are a lot of folks who wanted Travis gone, but not a lot who would actually kill him. Have you talked to Pete Quinn?"

"Not yet," Tj answered. "Do you think he might know something?"

"I don't know," Jeremy admitted. "Pete's a good guy, but he's been acting odd lately. It might be nothing, but if I was the one investigating things, I'd want to at least talk to the guy."

"So?" Kyle asked when Tj returned.

"He said he was working. I can verify that with his staff, but I'm inclined to believe him."

"He's one of the investors who got burned?"

"Yeah, along with Pete Quinn and a few others. Jeremy mentioned that Pete has been acting odd lately. He recommended I talk to him. I planned on going by his shop today, but I was too busy."

"We can hit him up tomorrow," Kyle said. "By the way, I talked to Kurt Brown while I was waiting for you." Kurt Brown, a local contractor, had been one of Tj's suspects during her investigation of the Zachary Collins murder. After he'd been cleared, Tj had hooked him up with Kyle, who'd needed a contractor to renovate the estate Zachary had left him. "He mentioned he was meeting with Murphy on Monday to discuss the repairs to the bar that resulted from the fight Travis started. It sounds like he was there during the time of death the medical examiner came up with, so I guess we can take Murphy off the list."

Tj took her phone out of her pocket, where she'd transferred the list they'd made the other evening. "If Jeremy's alibi checks out, that just leaves us with Johnson, Sean Wright, Albert Pitman, Coach Parker, and Pete Quinn from the original list. I added Josh, not because I think he did it but because we need to figure out where he is and why he left. I added Chelsea to the list as well. Again, I don't think she's guilty, but if we can figure out an alibi for her, maybe we can get her out of jail. Unfortunately, it looks like we've done about as much as we can do tonight."

CHAPTER 13

Thursday, February 20

"I know you're all nervous, but you've got this." Tj was nearing the end of her pre-meet motivational speech. "We rocked yesterday and we'll rock today. It's been a tough week with Sarah being out, but everyone has stepped up, and I know we can come out of this thing with enough points to rocket us into first place."

"Who's a winner?" Connor chanted.

"We're a winner," the team responded.

Tj watched as the kids gathered their gear and headed toward the ski lift. Although there were events going on in town, Tj and the kids had had a full day ahead of them on the hill. And what a day it had turned out to be. The sun was shining, the short storm they'd had late the previous evening had left a layer of fresh powder, and the excitement in the air had made her feel as if she were a kid again.

Tj gathered her own gear and headed toward the lift. A small part of her wished she were the one competing today, but in her heart she knew she'd had her moment as a competitor and it was now time to take a backseat and cheer on her team.

* * *

By lunch, the team was two points behind Beaver Creek. Connor had set a record best with his first run, and Brittany was shredding the mountain as if she had jet packs on her skis. Eric was a little off today, and in retrospect, she probably should have had him sit out. He'd sworn that he was fine and ready to ski, but a fall on his second run had cost the team the points they were going to need if they were going to beat Beaver Creek.

Tj sat with her kids when they gathered on the large outdoor deck for burgers before their afternoon heats. In spite of the fact that this was her favorite part of the day, she found her mind wandering. Chelsea was still in jail and, as she and Kyle had speculated the previous evening, it did seem that Boggs had put the kibosh on an aggressive effort to find another suspect. Besides that, Dennis was frantic to find Josh, who hadn't returned to his apartment in days and remained unaccounted for.

Tj had been avoiding Dylan because she didn't want to be put in the position of telling him about Josh until she was able to clear him, but she didn't want to lie to him either. She'd thought about it a lot in the past thirty-six hours and realized that if she couldn't locate Josh to ask him face to face what in the heck was going on, she'd need to find the killer before either Dylan or Boggs put two and two together.

Tj hadn't had a lot of time to investigate, but she had a little bit of time now; the next heat wasn't due to start for a couple of hours. There were a number of suspects right here on the mountain. She'd noticed both Coach Parker and Barney Johnson in the crowd during the morning races. Jeremy Young and Pete Quinn both owned businesses in the village. Chances were they'd be onsite during such a busy time. Albert Pitman, who owned the Inn, where Travis had been drinking in the bar before he'd been killed, was most likely around as well. She didn't know if she'd be able to trace the drugs he'd ingested back to the bar, but given the limited amount of time she had, it seemed an easy place to start.

"I need to run an errand," she said to Connor, who was sitting next to her. "I shouldn't be long, but if I'm late getting back, can you be sure everyone is suited up and ready to go for the giant slalom?"

"Yeah, no problem. Everything okay?"

Connor knew her well enough to be sure that in most cases she'd never put the needs of the team on competition day behind anything else. "I just need to talk to someone. It shouldn't take long."

"Okay." Connor smiled. "We'll see you on the hill, if not before."

Tj dumped her empty plate and paper cup into the garbage before heading back through the crowded snack bar toward the main artery connecting the various buildings in the ski village to one another. The complex had been redeveloped a few years earlier, and worn-out storefronts had been replaced by brand-new faces depicting a log-cabin theme. White lights were strung overhead, providing a fairy-tale feel after dark, and large portable fireplaces were set about so the after-ski crowd could enjoy a warm or cold drink under the night sky.

"Coach Long," Tj greeted Sean Wright's coach. Tj had seen both Sean and Long in the crowd during the races that had been held that morning. "Have you enjoyed the races?"

"I have. You've got a couple of kids on your team with real potential."

"They're a good group."

"I imagine coaching this age group is very rewarding."

"It is," Tj acknowledged. "Although I'm sure coaching a world-class boarder like Sean has its own rewards."

"I've been lucky enough to work with several fantastic snowboarders. Still, I can remember when my daughter Pamela was on the high-school team. There's something really special about cheering your own flesh and blood across the finish line."

"I love what I do. I can't claim to have any family to cheer on just yet, but the kids on my team are the closest thing. Does your daughter still compete?"

"No. She had a setback last spring and decided to retire."

"That's when you started working with Sean?"

"Sean approached me after my previous athlete, Walter Tovar, retired last summer."

"I've heard of him," Tj fished. "He was doing so well. Why did he quit? I seem to remember that many members of the snowboard community felt he was at the peak of his career."

Coach Long shrugged. "Walter had some personal issues he needed to deal with. I was lucky Sean was looking for a coach."

"Where is Sean? I saw the two of you together earlier."

"In the bar. I needed a break from all the noise and decided to get some fresh air."

"I don't blame you; the bar tends to get pretty crazy during carnival."

"Good luck this afternoon."

"Thanks. We're going to need it."

Long went on his way and Tj continued on toward the Inn, turning left, away from the bar, and heading down the wide hallway to the front desk. The lobby was one of Tj's favorite places on the mountain. Quaint and cozy, it provided the perfect backdrop for the fabulous views outside the large picture windows.

"Is Albert around?" Tj asked the middle-aged desk clerk.

"He's in his office. Do you have an appointment?"

"No. Can you tell him Tj Jensen is here to see him?"

"Certainly. If you can have a seat, I'll be right back with you."

Tj walked over to the window and looked out at the spectacular view. The lodge overlooked Joshua's Run, one of the most popular on the mountain. Hundreds of people wearing brightly colored skiwear zigzagged across the wide expanse of snow.

Tj couldn't remember the last time she'd come out to the resort simply to have some fun. She was out here almost every day during the season with the team, but the freedom that could be found as you meandered about wherever the mood took you could not be duplicated when you had drills to run and times to beat.

"It appears I was wrong about Mr. Pitman's whereabouts," the woman explained. "One of our employees called in sick, so he's in the main lobby, helping out at the ice-cream counter."

"Okay, thanks. I'll find him there."

Tj headed back toward the front of the building. She realized that striking up a conversation at the ice-cream counter would be a lot easier than trying to explain why she was requesting an audience in his office.

"Hey, Tj. What can I get you?" Albert asked as Tj walked up to the counter.

Tj considered her options. "A chocolate cone."

Albert began to scoop the dark brown ice cream.

"I'm surprised you're working the counter. It seems like you must be slammed in the lodge."

"We are. My niece Polly," he said, mentioning his eldest sister's daughter, who lived with them and helped out at the inn, "was supposed to work today, but she's had a bit of a setback."

Tj noticed that the light in Albert's eyes had been replaced with anger, and the muscles around his mouth clenched, as if he could barely contain his emotion. "We decided to send her home to stay with her mom for a spell."

"I hope everything's okay."

"It is now." The light returned to Albert's eyes. "That'll be four dollars."

Tj handed Albert a five-dollar bill. "I guess things must have calmed down a bit now that Travis isn't around to cause a ruckus."

"They have at that." Albert's smile didn't quite reach his eyes.

"It's a shame what happened," Tj tried.

"Oh, I don't know." Albert handed her back her change. "Seems to me the boy got what he deserved."

"Yeah, I guess." Tj shrugged. "I heard he was drugged before he was stabbed. Seems like more than one person decided to get payback for their rage."

"Drugged?" Albert paled.

"I don't suppose you remember who served him his drink?"

"No." Albert cleared his throat. "Can't say that I do. It's been busy, so everyone has been covering for everyone else. You don't think one of my servers did it?"

Tj shook her head, trying to act nonchalant in spite of the fact that Albert was seriously stressing over the direction of the conversation. "I'm pretty sure Boggs believes that Chelsea Hanson is the guilty party. I guess you heard they arrested her."

"Yeah." Albert looked toward the crowd forming behind her. "I heard."

"Seems odd to me that Travis ended up in his room," Tj continued. "Not much of a chance Chelsea could have moved him unless she had help from someone at the resort."

"Will that do it for yah?" Albert looked anxious for her to move on.

Tj turned around and looked at the line. "It seems you might need to bring in some more help."

"Tried to, but a couple of our regulars quit when they heard they might not get paid on time."

"Why wouldn't they get paid?"

"You must have heard about the fire at the admin building?"

"Of course."

"All kinds of sensitive paperwork was destroyed, including personnel and payroll records," Albert informed her. "There's been talk that the next payroll might be delayed while they sort everything out."

"Have you heard how the fire started?"

"No. There's a rumor that there was arson involved, but I haven't seen an official report. I just can't imagine who would do such a thing. There are a lot of people who are going to be hurting if they can't get the payroll out on time."

"The whole thing seems really odd, given everything else that's happened. I can't help but wonder if the fire wasn't in some way related to Travis Davidson's murder."

"What?" Albert looked genuinely shocked. "I don't see how it could be."

Tj shrugged. "I hope everything turns out okay with the payroll situation." She walked away, wanting to know a whole lot more but afraid to push her luck. It seemed apparent that Albert knew something that was causing him distress, but she couldn't put her finger on what that something might be. Maybe she'd come back and snoop around when she had more time.

*   *   *

Tj was headed back toward the ski area when she ran into Kyle. "What are you doing here?"

"I was in town helping with the family events, but I wanted to catch Connor's run this afternoon."

"He had fabulous times this morning."

"I sort of figured you'd be with the team."

"I wanted to question Albert Pitman. I think he might be involved in this whole mess."

"I don't know." Kyle frowned. "I realize we put him on the list because he complained to Mayor Wallaby about the disruptions Travis was causing, but honestly, I never really figured him for the killer."

"Yeah, me neither." Tj took another bite of her ice cream. "Initially, I just wanted to talk to him so I could cross him off the list and move on, but it feels like there might be something more going on."

"Such as?"

"Albert has a niece, Polly, who lives with the Pitmans and helps out at the Inn. Albert mentioned that she was supposed to work today but that something happened at the last minute to make him send her home for a visit with her mother."

"And this is important because..."

"Sarah told me that Chelsea mentioned that she wasn't the first person Travis had sexually assaulted. Polly is a cute girl who lives at the Inn. I imagine she came into contact with Travis when he was in town."

"So you think Travis assaulted Polly, Albert sent her home to her mother, and then he killed Travis?"

Tj shrugged. "I don't know. I guess it's farfetched, but Albert's entire demeanor changed when we talked about Polly.

And then, when I said I hoped everything was going to be okay, he got this strange look on his face and said 'it is now.' The whole conversation made the hair on the back of my neck stand on end.

"Besides," Tj added, as they neared the base lodge, "Dylan told me Travis was drugged before he left the bar. When I mentioned that to Albert, he looked like he was going to pass out. He has access to the emergency door and the service elevator. I'm not saying he's guilty of anything, but I do think he warrants further investigation."

"So what now?"

"I'm not sure. I need to get to the mountain. I guess I'll noodle on it for a while."

"Should we fill Dylan in?" Kyle asked.

Tj hesitated. "I don't know. Maybe we should keep this to ourselves for now. If we tell Dylan, he'll be obligated to talk to Albert, and I hate to pull him into this until after I have a chance to think about it a bit."

"Has anyone heard from Josh?"

"No. Dennis has called him a million times, but he hasn't answered or called back. He's getting really worried."

Kyle stopped walking and looked directly at her. "I realize Dylan is a cop, and as a cop he has certain responsibilities, but in the time I've known him, he's seemed like a pretty decent guy who's open to working outside the limits of protocol. If you believe that Josh is innocent, then chances are he's not on the run. If he's not on the run and isn't answering his phone, he could be in real trouble."

"You're right. I'll talk to Dylan later if I can track him down."

*   *   *

"Congratulations." Coach Parker came up and hugged Tj after the final heat, which had earned them enough points to take the first-place standing away from Beaver Creek.

"Thanks, although it's the kids who should be congratulated. They've made so much progress just this week."

"I know. I've been keeping an eye on them," Parker informed her. "Especially Connor Harrington. I met with Sean Wright on Monday, and he's seriously considering mentoring Harrington if he's interested in breaking into the pro circuit. His new coach is onboard as well. One of his stipulations is that a few of us agree to work with him for the remainder of the year."

Tj remembered the meeting she'd witnessed between Sean Harris, Johnson, and Coach Parker in the bar on Monday afternoon.

"That would be fantastic. I know Connor wants to go to college, but a chance to hit the pro circuit would be a huge opportunity."

"For both of us. I've been looking for someone to take on ever since Travis left."

"I was sorry to hear about what happened." Coach Parker had been burned by Travis, but the two of them had been like father and son at one point. The fact that he'd been murdered must have hurt.

"Yeah." Parker looked genuinely sad. "Travis was a good kid. I don't know what happened to him, and I admit to having been angry with him after how he treated everyone, but I can't help but remember the good times as well. He was such a cocky kid. When we first started working together, he was full of raw talent but short on discipline. Sometimes I wonder if we did the right thing by coddling him all those years. I guess he didn't have what it took to handle his success. It ended up turning him into something he might otherwise never have been. I know he'd been acting like a first-class ass recently, but he didn't deserve this. During the past few days, I've found myself wishing I'd gone after him when he ran out of the bar. I almost did. I stood up to follow him, but I realized I'd be late picking up my daughter from dance, so I turned around and headed toward the parking lot instead. I can't help but wonder if Travis would still be alive if I hadn't had carpool duty that day. I hope they find whoever did this to him."

"I'm sure they will."

Tj checked Coach Parker off her list. The man seemed genuinely distraught, and it would be easy enough to verify that he had indeed picked up his daughter from her class. She needed to get going, but it would only take a few minutes to talk to Jeremy Young and Pete Quinn if they were in their shops.

CHAPTER 14

After she left the mountain, Tj headed into town to catch up with Kyle and then try to track down Dylan. Kyle was right, she had no reason not to trust Dylan to do the right thing with the information she'd managed to gather. Kyle was waiting for her near the town center. They found Dylan at the food court taking a break.

"I had a visitor this afternoon," Dylan said after ordering a sandwich. "He confessed to drugging Travis the day he was killed and attributed his decision to turn himself in to a conversation he had with you."

"Albert Pitman," Tj guessed.

"Good guess. How did you know?"

"I ran into him at lunch today, and he mentioned that his niece had made an unplanned trip home to visit her mother due to some emotional turmoil. I knew Travis was staying at the Inn, and Chelsea told Sarah that she wasn't the first girl he had sexually abused. I figured that Polly, who I know is a friend of Chelsea's, must have been the girl she was referring to. I figure the rape of a family member is about as good a reason to kill someone as anything."

"An excellent theory that's actually close to what really happened," Dylan congratulated her. "Except that Polly wasn't raped and Albert didn't kill Travis."

"Okay." Tj was intrigued. "Then what did happen?"

"As you might guess, Travis has been a thorn in Albert's side since the day he checked in. Not only has he disturbed the other guests but he's been rude to his staff, and although he didn't rape Polly, he did seem to take a disturbing sort of glee in harassing her. Albert complained to the mayor, who told him in no uncertain terms that Travis was in town for an important meeting and under no circumstances could he kick him out. I guess Mayor Wallaby offered to compensate Albert generously for the inconvenience, but he didn't want Polly to go through any more grief, so he sent her to visit her mother.

"After Polly left," Dylan continued, "Travis became even more obnoxious than he had been before, so Albert once again complained to the mayor. I don't know the actual details because Albert refused to supply them, but I guess the mayor has something he's holding over Albert's head, which created a situation in which Albert couldn't simply kick Travis out. The more Albert thought about it, the madder he became at both Travis and Mayor Wallaby. He let his anger stew until he'd developed an uncontrollable urge to get even."

Tj was itching to cut through the details and get on with the story, but for once in her life she decided to hold her tongue and let Dylan finish uninterrupted.

"Albert decided that the best way to get back at both Travis and Mayor Wallaby was to prevent Travis from attending the meeting that seemed to be so important to both men."

"So he slipped something into his drink," Tj realized.

"Exactly," Dylan confirmed. "He figured he'd start to feel woozy and head up to his room. By the time Travis came to, he would have missed his important meeting and Albert would have gotten his revenge."

"But Chelsea came in and messed everything up," Kyle guessed. "Travis followed her out of the bar, and I imagine

Albert felt obligated to follow after them as well, to ensure that Travis didn't come to any real harm."

"He did," Dylan verified.

"So why didn't he report what happened in the locker room?" Kyle wondered.

"Because he'd have to admit his own role in the affair," Tj said.

"Exactly." Dylan nodded. "He said he waited around until Chelsea and Sarah left, and made sure there was no real danger from the stab wound. He decided to let Travis sleep it off in his room, so he got the wheelchair and covered Travis with a blanket to hide the blood. He accessed the Inn thorough the back entrance, so no one even saw him come in. Then he used Travis's room key, which was in his shirt pocket, to get into his room and put him safely into his bed."

"So why did Albert confess now?"

"When he found out Travis was dead, he realized he might actually be responsible," Dylan continued. "When he spoke to Tj, he realized she was suspicious of him. According to Albert, Tj is like a dog with a bone when she sets her mind to something, and if she'd set her mind to uncovering what happened, it would only be a matter of time. He decided I'd go easier on him if he turned himself in and confessed his involvement."

"And will you?" Kyle asked. "Go easier on him, I mean?"

"It's not really up to me. The guy knowingly drugged a man, something that may or may not have contributed to his death. He's being transported to the larger county jail in Indulgence as we speak. It's hard to say what the district attorney will do, but I'd be willing to bet he'll take Albert's cooperation into account."

"I just thought of something," Tj blurted.

Dylan smiled. "I was wondering how long it would take you to figure it out."

"Figure what out?" Kyle asked.

"Albert said he went into the locker room after Sarah and Chelsea left. He verified that Travis was alive before moving him *and* verified that Travis still had his room key, so Chelsea couldn't have taken it and snuck in later," Tj explained.

"So Chelsea couldn't have killed him," Kyle finished.

"Has Chelsea been released?" Tj asked.

"Not yet," Dylan said. "Boggs is dragging his feet, but I think Albert's testimony will be enough to convince a judge to let her out on bail at the very least. I'd be willing to bet she'll be sleeping in her own bed tonight."

Tj took a deep breath of relief. "Thanks for taking the time to tell me this."

"I figured you'd want to know. Now that I've shared it with you, I was hoping you might be inclined to share with me what you know," Dylan prompted.

"I talked to Coach Parker and Jeremy Young," Tj answered. "They both appear to have alibis, so I think we can take them off the list."

"I concur," Dylan agreed. "I spoke to them as well."

"I guess that leaves Johnson, Sean Wright, and Pete Quinn," Kyle said.

"Barney Johnson loathed Travis Davidson about as much as I've ever seen a man loathe another, but as far as I can tell, he's not our guy," Dylan asserted.

"No?"

"He claims he was in the bar talking to Sean Wright and a few others, but then he left to head over to Mayor Wallaby's office. He spent the next hour threatening to have him removed from office. I checked with the mayor, who corroborated his story."

"Which gives Mayor Wallaby an alibi as well," Tj concluded.

"Sort of," Dylan answered.

"Why would the mayor need an alibi?" Kyle asked. "Isn't he the one who brought Travis here in the first place?"

"Yeah, but word around the Antiquery, where I get most of my gossip," Dylan teased, "is that he was partnered with him in some sort of business deal. What if the deal went sour?"

"You hang out at the Antiquery to catch up on the latest gossip?" Tj had to ask.

"Certainly. Serenity is a small town. The best way to keep tabs on what's *really* going on is to have a cup of coffee and listen to the chatter of the women who make it their business to know everything there is to know. I stop by almost every day."

Tj laughed. "Now I've heard everything. So you said the meeting *sort of* gave the men an alibi?"

"Just to be certain that the double alibi wasn't intentional, I mentioned the meeting to Harriet, who I ran into at the Antiquery this morning, and she confirmed that it was a lively meeting indeed. Based on the time of death and the distance from town to Angel Mountain, either man could have returned to the mountain and killed Travis after the argument."

"Did the men say where they went after their argument?" Tj wondered.

"Johnson said he went home. Unfortunately, he was alone in the house, so we don't have anyone to verify his statement. Tim and Roy are questioning neighbors. We figure that someone might have seen him come home."

"And Mayor Wallaby?" Tj asked.

"The good mayor is being a bit more evasive. He said he went to visit a friend, but he won't divulge the name of that person. I told him that I couldn't completely clear him as a suspect, and he said he wasn't worried about it because he didn't do it, and once we find the real killer, he'll be cleared anyway."

"Mayor Wallaby has a way with the women," Tj said. "He seems to prefer married women. He's most likely protecting his newest mistress."

"What about Sean Wright?" Kyle asked. "It seems he has the most to gain with Travis out of the way."

"Sean was in the bar at Angel Mountain during the time Chelsea and Travis fought. He told me that he witnessed the altercation, had another drink, and left shortly after they did. He claims he went directly back to your resort. I checked with members of the staff. A few remembered seeing Sean in the bar at around eight, but since we estimate that Travis died between five and seven, that doesn't really help him. Sean would have had plenty of time to kill Travis and still be at the bar by eight."

"And no one else remembered seeing him?" Tj wondered.

"Not that we've been able to find out so far."

"I guess that does it for now."

"Are you sure you haven't uncovered anything else?" Dylan asked.

Tj hesitated. The last thing she wanted to do was make Dennis or Jenna mad, and if Dylan handled her news in the wrong way, mad was exactly what they'd be. On the other hand, she'd never known him to be anything but fair, and she had no reason to believe he wouldn't handle the situation with sensitivity.

"It's about the fire at Angel Mountain," Tj began.

"You mean the fire Travis started in order to destroy the evidence Pete Quinn has been using to blackmail him?"

"Pete Quinn has been blackmailing Travis?" Tj asked. "How do you know that?"

"I'm a cop," Dylan pointed out. "I go out and investigate. What did you think I was doing all day while you were coaching races and questioning suspects?"

Tj actually blushed. It really hadn't occurred to her that Dylan might turn up evidence in her absence.

"So why was Pete blackmailing Travis, what did he have on him, and how is it related to the murder?" Tj asked.

"As you've already informed me," Dylan said, "Pete Quinn invested a lot of money in Travis only to have him renege on his agreement to act as a spokesperson for him after he made a name for himself. To make matters worse, Travis announced that he was in negotiation with Pete's biggest competitor. It turned out Pete knew that Travis had taken steroids prior to last year's nationals. Coach Parker wanted to cover it up, and Pete somehow helped him to falsify the official records. The original drug results were kept in a file in the admin office because Travis was still on the Angel Mountain team at the time, and Pete used his knowledge of them to blackmail Travis after he bailed on him."

"So Travis met with sponsors and Pete used the files to threaten Travis if he signed with his competitor," Tj guessed.

"Exactly. Travis didn't have access to the file, so he decided to burn down the whole building," Dylan confirmed.

"How do you know that for sure?" Kyle asked. "Travis is dead, and dead men don't talk."

"I know it because a nice chap by the name of Josh Steinbeck told me that Travis had told him as much."

"You talked to Josh?" Tj asked.

"This afternoon," Dylan confirmed.

"But how did you know to talk to him?"

"I tracked Josh down to the hospital in Sacramento where his father is being treated for third-degree burns."

"So that's where he's been." Tj sighed in relief. "We've been trying to get hold of him, but he isn't answering his cell or returning calls."

"He told me that he dropped his phone at some point and hasn't been able to find it. He used the pay phone in the hospital to call in to work and had no idea anyone was looking for him."

"Okay, let's back up," Tj said, trying to wrap her head around the whole thing. "How exactly did *you* find Josh?"

"After my source from the bar told me about Josh's reaction after receiving the phone call on Sunday evening, I decided to have a chat with him. The first place I looked was at the firehouse. They told me that he'd called in requesting time off for personal reasons. When he wasn't at home and didn't answer his cell, I pulled the phone records for the day and time Josh called the firehouse and found out the call originated from a hospital in Sacramento. I called the hospital and had him paged. Once I got hold of him, he was quite helpful."

"So we know that Travis called Josh on Sunday and confessed to starting the fire, and we also know that the man who was burned in the fire is Josh's biological father," Tj said. "We can assume that when Travis found out the man was injured, he felt bad and called Josh to apologize. What we don't know is how Travis knew Bert was Josh's dad."

"Travis knew Bert was Josh's father because Bert is also Travis's father," Dylan informed her.

"What?" Tj was stunned. "Josh and Travis are brothers?"

"Half-brothers," Dylan confirmed.

Tj had known that Josh's biological father had had an affair that resulted in the birth of a child. That child must have been Travis. After Josh's mother divorced Bert, he'd taken off and hadn't been heard from for years. More recently, he'd returned to Serenity to try to establish a relationship with his son. It made sense that he'd have been in contact with both of his sons, and that they knew of each other's existence.

"Let me get this straight," Tj began. "Josh and Travis are

half-brothers. Travis set the fire at Angel Mountain to destroy the records relating to his drug test, but I'm assuming he didn't intend for anyone to get hurt. Bert, who was working in another building, saw the smoke and went to investigate. He tried to put out the fire with a hose while he was waiting for the fire department, but what he didn't know was that someone had carelessly left dynamite from the recent avalanche control in the back room. The dynamite blows and Bert was seriously injured."

"Travis, coldhearted bastard that he was," Tj continues, "actually felt bad about what happened to Bert and called Josh to confess. When Josh heard that Travis was responsible for Bert's injuries, he took off to confront him. Then what?" she asked. "How did he end up in Sacramento?"

"While he was on his way to Angel Mountain, he received a call from the hospital. The doctor he talked to told him that Bert's injuries were serious enough that they were airlifting him to Sacramento. It looked like he might lose an arm, so Josh decided it was more important to be with his father during the surgery than it was to beat the snot out of his brother. He changed direction and headed down the hill."

"And somewhere along the way he lost his phone, so he used the pay phone in the hospital to call into work, never knowing that anyone was worried about him," Tj finished.

"On the bright side, he has an alibi for Travis's murder on Monday," Kyle pointed out.

"Yeah," Tj nodded, "there's that." She looked directly at Dylan, "I'm sorry. I should have told you about Josh right away."

"Why didn't you?" said Dylan disappointedly.

"I don't know. Josh is Dennis's best friend. On the surface, it looked like Josh might have killed Travis. I was afraid if I told you, you'd feel obligated to arrest him. I should have given you more credit."

"I wouldn't have arrested him without cause," Dylan reminded her.

"I know. I'm sorry. I shouldn't have kept this from you. It won't happen again. Forgive me?"

"We'll see."

"So what now?" Tj asked.

"We know who stabbed Travis, and who drugged him," Kyle said while Dylan and Tj sat looking at each other. "I guess we just need to figure out who actually killed him."

CHAPTER 15

Friday February 21

Tj awoke on Friday morning to snow flurries in the air. The local weather report predicted the high for the day would be a blustery twenty-eight degrees. She pulled on an old wool robe over the long johns she'd worn to bed. Slipping her feet into knee-high slippers, she stumbled into the bathroom attached to her bedroom and turned on the small space heater. Splashing cold water on her face in an attempt to wake up, she went downstairs and into a thankfully toasty warm kitchen.

Tj wasn't certain what time Ben got up in the morning, but nine times out of ten he had the coffee made, breakfast started, and the room warm from the crackling fire before anyone else in the house had emerged from the bedrooms upstairs. She opened the door and let Echo out for his early morning romp. After filling the cat dishes with fresh food and water, she poured herself a cup of hot coffee before snagging one of the freshly baked cinnamon rolls Ben had left cooling on the counter.

"What time are we leaving for the carnival?" Ashley appeared before Tj could take her first bite of the hot roll dripping with melted frosting.

"I told Jenna I'd help out at the sled-dog races, since they canceled the downhill events scheduled for today, and they start at nine, so I guess we should leave here by eight." Tj glanced at the clock, which read 6:24.

"Ice fishing is at ten," Ben reminded her.

"I know. I figure I'll help Jenna with the sled dogs and then use the snowmobile to cut a direct path to Miller's Pond. I should be there in time to help you get set up."

"How about us?" Gracie asked. "Can we snowmobile with you?"

"Sorry, sweetie, not this time. Papa is going to bring you in the truck. Where is he, anyway?"

"Right here." Mike walked in through the kitchen door, with Echo on his heels. Both man and dog were covered in freshly fallen snow. "I wanted to check to make sure everything was set for today's activities. The resort is hosting the Silly but Awesome contest."

Every year, Maggie's Hideaway sponsored a fun event for those visitors who wanted to participate but weren't into serious competition. The activities director had dubbed the event the Silly but Awesome competition, and even had t-shirts for all participants, as well as a trophy for the overall winner. This year, the resort had organized a triathlon of sorts, including a snowshoe race in which each contestant had to carry a tray filled with drinks while walking as quickly as they could wearing the oversized shoes, a paintball-type event using colored snowballs and Nerf guns, and an ice-hockey-type event in which teams were given five chances to make a goal from midcourt with only a man dressed as a giant brown bear as the goalie.

"But we don't want to go in the truck," Gracie argued. "We want to go with you on the snowmobile."

"Yeah," Ashley joined in. "How come Tj gets to go on the snowmobile and we can't?"

"Because," Mike kissed each of the girls on the top of the head before taking off his hat and gloves, "we're going to the carnival in style."

"Style?" Ashley asked.

"The resort is offering sleigh rides during the carnival this year, so I decided to hook the horses up a little early and take my two best girls into town."

"We're going to the carnival in the sleigh?" Both girls screamed with excitement.

"I told Rosalie we'd pick her up at seven forty-five, so I need you to finish your breakfast and get dressed."

The girls jumped out of their chairs and ran across the kitchen to hug Mike, who was pouring a cup of coffee. It warmed Tj's heart, the way her dad had embraced her sisters and accepted them into his life. At first Tj had thought it might be strange for him to be put in the position of raising his ex-wife's children by another man. But, in the end, he'd never shown even the tiniest hesitation in making them part of the family.

"We'll go *only* after you finish breakfast and are dressed in warm clothes, including your snowsuits, boots, hats, and gloves," Mike warned the girls.

"Breakfast is ready." Ben set a platter with eggs, bacon, hash browns, and toast in the center of the table, next to the mostly empty platter of cinnamon rolls. "I've already eaten, so I'm going to head upstairs. Doc and Bookman are going to pick me up in half an hour. We still need to get the ice-fishing house placed over the hole we cut yesterday."

"You fish in a house?" Gracie asked.

"It's really a small hut with a bench to sit on and a hole in the floor that you position over the hole you cut in the ice. It helps to keep you warm."

"Can I see it?" Gracie asked.

"Tj can bring you out onto the ice on the snowmobile when she gets there."

"We can't go until we find Crissy," Gracie stated.

"Crissy is missing?" Tj asked.

"No one has seen her since yesterday," Ashley responded.

"She's been acting funny," Gracie added.

"Funny how?" Tj wondered.

"She's been walking around and meowing, and she wouldn't eat her dinner last night. I took her in my room when I went to bed, but she was gone when I woke up."

Tj had been meaning to take Crissy to Rosalie for a checkup ever since they'd adopted her, but she seemed to have gained weight and looked to be healthy, and Tj'd been so busy, she hadn't gotten around to it. Gracie, who'd adopted the cat as her own the minute Tj had brought her home from Zachary's house, would be crushed if something happened to her new friend. It had only been six months since her mom's death. The last thing she needed was to lose something she loved.

"You girls finish your breakfast and then get dressed. I'll look for her," Tj promised. "She probably just found a comfy place to hide and is sleeping in."

"I don't blame her for looking for another place to sleep. Gracie kicks in her sleep," Ashley commented.

"Do not."

"Do so."

"It doesn't matter," Tj intervened. "You each have your own room and your own bed now, and I'm sure Crissy loves sleeping with Gracie. She probably snuck out for a snack when I went in to check on you guys last night and then couldn't get back in after I closed the door. I'm sure she's fine. Now hurry up and finish your breakfasts."

* * *

Tj waved to Jenna as she maneuvered her way through the throngs of people gathered to watch the sled-dog races. While many of the participants owned their own teams, Dennis had borrowed one from Maddie Crawford, an eccentric old woman who lived outside of town with the twenty-six dogs she bred and raced. Dennis and Maddie first became friends when he was just ten years old. He'd been out ice fishing when he saw one of her dogs that was chasing a rabbit fall through the ice. Dennis had rescued the pup at great risk to his own safety, and Maddie had been trying to pay him back for his heroic deed ever since. Dennis wouldn't take money as a reward, but he'd always wanted to learn how to manage a team, so Maddie had taken him under her wing, and Dennis had placed in the top three during each of the past five winter carnivals.

"You're late," Jenna commented.

"I was looking for Crissy."

"Something happened to Crissy?"

"I hope not. She didn't come down for breakfast this morning, and Gracie said she didn't sleep with her last night. She's slept with Gracie every night since we brought her home."

"I hope she's okay," Jenna worried.

"Me too. Gracie will be heartbroken if something happens to that cat. Ashley remembers seeing her yesterday, and Gracie said she didn't eat her dinner last night. She took her to bed with her, but she was gone when she woke up this morning."

"Maybe you should have Rosalie take a look at her when you track her down," Jenna suggested.

"I've been meaning to do that. She probably needs her shots, but I've been so busy, I haven't gotten around to asking."

"I wouldn't worry. Cats are independent souls. I'm sure

she'll turn up," Jenna assured her. "Oh, look, they're getting ready to start."

"Is the dog on the left new?" Tj asked.

Jenna nodded. "They've only been working together for a month, but Dennis is very excited about his chances this year."

Tj crossed the first two fingers on each of her hands. "Here's hoping. What happened to Maddie's arm?"

The woman, who usually won the competition every year, had entered her own team as usual, but she had a cast on her arm.

"Dennis said she had a fall."

"And she's going to run her dogs anyway?" Tj asked.

"Apparently. You know Maddie. It'll take more than a broken arm to slow her down. Is Kyle coming out for the race?" Jenna wondered.

"He has the Silly but Awesome competition this morning. He said he'd meet up with us afterward. Where are your girls?"

"Your dad picked them up in the sleigh. I took a picture of the four girls all bundled up on the backseat while your dad drove and Rosalie sat next to him. It's really cute. I'll forward you a copy."

"Taking photos is one thing I need to get better about doing," Tj admitted. "All my friends who have kids have a phone full of pictures of the little darlings, and I have maybe five."

"Most parents start off taking photos of their adorable new baby. There's this almost manic drive to capture every first: first smile, first step, first tooth. Once they get going, they get into the habit. Remember all the photos you took of Echo when he was a pup?"

Tj did remember. Her friends were as sick of looking at puppy pictures as she was of looking at photos of babies.

"It looks like they're getting ready to start," Jenna said.

"Let's work our way to the front. I want to get a picture of Dennis crossing the finish line."

Dennis did well, but he couldn't beat Maddie Crawford despite her injury. Watching the woman work with her team was something to behold. She knew exactly what to do and when to do it to get the optimum performance from the dogs, who obviously adored the ground she walked on. Tj had heard stories of sled-dog owners who treated their dogs like livestock, but to Maddie they were family.

As planned, Tj traveled cross-country on the snowmobile in order to get to the ice-fishing competition with enough time to help Ben position his warming hut over the hole he'd already carved in the ice. Dennis and Jenna promised to meet her at the event after Dennis helped Maddie transport the dogs and equipment to her house.

Ben was dressed like an Eskimo in a blizzard, but Tj knew once the competition began, the layers would start to work their way into a discard pile on the bench of the hut. Working a large fish through a small hole took a lot of muscle and tended to work up quite a sweat if things went well. The rules of the event dictated that the teams could aid each other in retrieving the fish they caught, but no one else could assist in any way. Tj doubted that Ben and Bonnie would win the event. For one thing, Bonnie wouldn't be joining Ben until halfway through the competition; for another, neither really had the upper-body strength to pull in a large catch even if they managed to snag one. There were prizes for both size and overall number caught, so maybe they could place in the numbers category.

"Did you see Grandpa's house?" Gracie trotted up to Tj. "It looks like a real house, only there's a big hole in the floor."

"I've seen it before," Tj confirmed. "I need to go to help Grandpa position his house in just the right place and then I'll come back and get you girls and take you for a ride out to see it up close."

"Okay," Ashley agreed. "We'll wait right here with Papa until you get back."

Ben had cut twin holes in what he believed to be a hot bed of fish activity. He'd been a fisherman all his life and knew the best places to throw a line, so he was hoping for a bountiful catch. It took the combined effort of Tj, Ben, and Bookman to maneuver the hut out onto the ice. Doc was busy preparing his chowder for the upcoming cook-off. After everything was in place, Tj ferried Ashley, Gracie, Kristi, and Kari out to the hut, giving each a chance to sit on the bench and watch how it was done.

"How'd the Silly but Awesome hockey go?" Tj asked Kyle when he arrived with Maggie's Hideaway activities director Julie Sorenson on his arm.

"Second place," he said, beaming.

"Congratulations." Tj hugged Kyle. "How are the rest of the events at the resort coming along?" she asked Julie.

"Fantastic. I have to get back for the snowmobile finals this afternoon, but Kyle offered to buy me lunch, and I had to eat."

"After all the long hours you've been putting in, you deserve a nice long lunch and more."

"Your dad said I could take the first two weeks of March off. I thought I'd go home and visit my family."

"I enjoyed meeting them last summer. You should definitely invite them out again," Tj suggested. The previous summer, Mike had comped a two-week stay for Julie's entire family. It had given the busy activities director a chance to visit her family without having to take time away from the resort during the busy season, and her family the opportunity to spend two weeks in one of the most beautiful places on the planet.

"I will. My mom and dad had a blast sailing and hiking, and my brothers still haven't stopped talking about parasailing and waterskiing."

"How's the fishing going?" Kyle asked.

"They're just about ready to start. I wanted to be here to wish Grandpa well, but once the event gets underway, it's really pretty boring."

"Julie and I are heading to the food court if you want to come along."

Tj hesitated. If Julie was expecting a romantic lunch, she wouldn't appreciate Tj's presence.

"Yeah, come with us," Julie encouraged. "I need to talk to you about the awards ceremony this afternoon. We can talk while we eat."

"Okay. I'll find out what Dennis and Jenna are doing and meet you there."

CHAPTER 16

After lunch, Tj and Kyle headed over to the toboggan race, which was held each year on the bunny hill, a moderately steep part of the slope that had been cleared of trees and gradually flattened out as it neared a parking area, where spectators lined up to watch. The toboggans started at the top of the hill, and each was given a place for the next run based on their order at the finish line. There were five heats, with toboggans eliminated after each one.

Since the toboggans were hand built by the teams, they came in a variety of shapes and colors. Most were designed to enhance speed, but every year a few were built for fun. Most of the entrants who chose to be overly creative didn't make it beyond the first run, but fun was had by all as sleds made to resemble outhouses, bathtubs, or spaceships sped down the hill.

"Does anyone know what number Helen and Bookman are?" Tj asked the group that had gathered to watch the race.

"I think Mom said they were in the middle of the pack," Jenna answered.

"Is that them?" Dennis pointed to a shiny sled that looked a lot like a rocket.

"Grandma has her red coat on," Kristi offered helpfully.

"Yeah, I think that's them." Kyle held a pair of binoculars up to his eyes.

"Can we see?" Gracie asked.

Kyle handed her the black glasses.

"Wow, here they come," Ashley cheered excitedly.

"I can't believe Mom wanted to do this." Jenna held her breath. "Those sleds are really cooking. It's a miracle no one ever gets really hurt."

"One of the guys broke his arm last year," Dennis pointed out. "And another had to have eight stitches put in his forehead the year before that."

"Not helping," Jenna growled as the first sleds reached the bottom of the hill.

"Relax." Dennis put his large arms around his wife. "The rocket ship has reached the bottom of the hill. It looks like they might have placed."

Jenna let out the breath she'd been holding.

"Which means they can go again," Kari cheered.

Helen and Bookman ended up getting in three runs before the more serious sleds took over for the final two heats. Although they didn't win, Helen said she'd had the time of her life and would do it again. After the competition, Dennis and Jenna decided to take all four girls ice skating while Helen and Bookman headed over to the ice fishing to check on Ben. Tj and Kyle wanted to follow up on a couple of ideas they'd had regarding the murder investigation, so they migrated toward the chowder cook-off to cheer on Doc and question celebrity judge Sean Wright.

"Looks like Dolly is making another appearance," Kyle commented as they headed toward the roped-off area where the contestants had set up booths in the multipurpose room of the community center.

Tj looked across the room to a table where the woman sat reading. As she'd been every other time she'd seen her, she was dressed in what Tj had come to think of as her Dolly costume. "It's so weird how she roams around town, picking random places to read."

"What if she's not reading in random places?" Kyle suggested.

"Huh?"

"What if she's strategically picking the locations where she's sitting for some reason unbeknownst to us?"

"Oh, I get it. Like maybe she's watching someone and she thinks sitting around in that ridiculous getup makes her inconspicuous."

"Exactly." Kyle grabbed Tj's arm and pulled her out of the way of a group of little boys who were barreling through the room.

"If Bookman was here, he'd make up a story about it," Tj replied.

"A story?"

"When I was ten, Dad, Grandpa, Bookman, and I went to San Francisco during one of Bookman's visits. While we were in the city, a bike messenger came around a corner and almost slammed into my dad. He jumped out of the way, but unfortunately, he ended up in the street, where he was hit by a taxi. Luckily, he wasn't really hurt all that bad, but the hospital wanted to keep him overnight for observation since he'd hit his head and blacked out for a minute. My grandpa went in to visit my dad, but they said I was too young, so Bookman waited in the lobby with me. I was bored and tired and scared, so to keep me entertained while we waited, we started picking out people who were also waiting, and making up stories about them. It sort of became our thing. In fact, we still do it sometimes."

"And if you were going to make up a story about this woman..."

Tj looked at her for a moment before she began. "She's a really incompetent spy, like a female Inspector Clouseau from the *Pink Panther* movies. She thinks that the ridiculous outfit she's wearing is a clever disguise."

"She's been following someone around town using the cover of pretending to read in order not to have her true motive revealed," Kyle said, playing along. "She's been watching..."

"Sean," Tj finished.

"Sean?"

"It has to be Sean," Tj insisted. "The first time I saw her was at the resort. She was reading in the lobby. The only other people in the room were Sean, his coach, Roger Long, two men from the International Ski Corporation, and a woman looking out of the window. The next time I saw her was in the Grill. It was lunch time and the room was packed, so I can't name everyone in the room, but Sean and his entourage were definitely at a table in the corner."

"And when we saw her in the bar at Angel Mountain, Sean was sitting at a table behind us," Kyle remembered.

Tj quickly went through the sightings she remembered in her head: the resort, the Antiquery, Angel Mountain, other venues throughout town. Without fail, Sean was nearby every time Dolly made an appearance. "Do you think the woman is really following Sean?" Tj wondered.

Kyle looked from the woman, who was still reading, to Sean, who was talking with his coach and Mayor Wallaby near the front of the building. "I don't know. Maybe," he mused. "Still, Sean seems unconcerned, and if the woman really had been following him everywhere, don't you think he would have noticed? I mean, she stands out like a sore thumb."

"Yeah, you're right. It's probably just a coincidence. Let's go find Doc to see if he needs any help. We won't have a chance to talk to Sean until after the judging, so we might as well try to make ourselves useful."

"Perfect timing." Doc beamed as Tj and Kyle walked up. "It's time to pour in the cream, but I knocked over the carton and spilled most of it. I was about to run next door to the mini-mart to buy a carton, but I hated to leave my masterpiece unattended."

"I'll go," Kyle volunteered. "Light, regular, or heavy?"

"Heavy. And get the big carton."

"That smells good," Tj said as Kyle headed toward the door.

"I went through my recipe book after we talked the other day and decided to make my grandmother's special seafood chowder. We used to make it every summer. I grew up in Los Angeles, but Mayma lived in Maine, in a beautiful place right on the seashore." Doc smiled. "Making our special recipe brought back a lot of beautiful memories, so I figure I'm a winner whether the judges agree or not."

Tj kissed Doc on the cheek. "That's why I love you. You're not only funny and sweet but you have a sentimental side that you aren't afraid to share with the world."

"I love you too, sweetheart. Hand me that big spoon."

Tj passed him the spoon.

"How'd Helen and Bookman do in the toboggan race?" he asked.

"They made it to the third round."

"Good for them. I would have loved to have been there to cheer them on, but making chowder is a daylong affair. Have you heard from Ben and Bonnie?"

"Bookman and Helen headed over after they finished their race. The derby should be about over. I imagine they'll all make their way over here when they're done. What time does the judging start?" Tj asked.

"Should be in half an hour or so. They had to postpone because one of the judges didn't show."

"Who didn't show?"

"Wendy Wells," Doc said, mentioning a woman who worked in the Inn. "I heard she had some sort of personal emergency."

Later that evening, Tj stood with a crowd, cheering on Mike and Rosalie as they skated to a waltz.

In all the years she'd known her, Tj had never realized Rosalie was a fan of ice dancing, and the only time her dad ever strapped on a pair of skates was to mix it up with the guys on the hockey team.

"They're really good," Tj shouted to Jenna as the crowd went wild with applause.

"I know," she yelled back. "I would never have expected them to enter this competition in a million years. Not that your dad isn't an excellent hockey player, and Rosalie is in really good shape, it's just that..."

"Yeah, I get it." Tj whistled in appreciation as the couple executed a perfectly orchestrated dip. "I'm as shocked as anyone."

"Did you see what Papa just did?" Ashley was clapping louder than anyone.

"I must say Mike looks distinguished in his tux," Helen complimented.

"And Rosalie is beautiful in her dress," Bonnie added. "I'm

not certain I've ever seen her in anything but sturdy pants and a cotton shirt."

"Oh, wow, did you see that?" Kristi gasped. "Can I take ice dancing lessons?"

"Me too," Ashley joined in.

"You're already pretty busy," Jenna cautioned.

"Can we at least get the information?" Kristi pleaded.

"I'll look into it," Jenna conceded, "but I'm not promising anything."

"Can we go to the sledding hill?" Gracie was somewhat less awed by the ice dancing than the older girls.

"As soon as this event is over," Tj promised.

"Can we get ice cream?" Kari asked.

"It's too cold for ice cream," Jenna replied as the crowd launched into a new round of applause when the dance came to an end.

"But I'm hungry," Kari insisted.

"Me too," Gracie said, deciding to ditch the sledding-hill effort in favor of a sweet snack.

"Bonnie and I will take the girls over to the ice-cream parlor if you want to finish watching the rest of the show," Helen said.

"Can we?" Gracie and Kari begged in unison.

Jenna looked at Tj, who nodded.

"Okay, but only one scoop each," Jenna instructed.

"We'll go with you," Ben added as he joined Bookman and Doc, who got up and followed the group across the street.

"Not that I don't appreciate a good waltz," Dennis put his arm around his wife, "but the guys from the station are heading over to Murphy's."

Jenna hesitated.

"Go ahead," Tj offered. "I'll take the older girls to the sledding hill after we finish here."

"I'll go with you," Kyle offered.

"If you're sure..." Jenna wasn't one to impose, no matter how many favors Tj owed her.

"We're sure."

Once the group had dwindled down, Tj felt her mind wandering. Watching the other contestants in the competition didn't have the same energizing affect as watching her dad and Rosalie. "Maybe we should head over to the hill now," she suggested. "There's bound to be a line."

"I'm game," Kyle assented.

"Girls?" Tj asked.

"Yeah, let's go," Ashley agreed.

As the foursome walked down the crowded street, she couldn't help but be impressed with the effort the town went to each year to put on a spectacular event. Bonfires were lit along the beach as couples, snuggled close for warmth, strolled along the waterline to enjoy the solitude that couldn't be found along the sidewalk lined with the mom-and-pop shops that made up Serenity's quaint downtown. The air was filled with delicious smells as street vendors sold delicious snacks of all kinds, and the band in the gazebo could be heard from several blocks away.

"I'll say one thing about this town," Kyle commented. "They certainly are into their festivals and celebrations. I've been here three and a half months and this is the fourth celebration I've been to."

"The holidays are always busy, but yeah, we do tend to overdo it a bit."

An hour later, Tj waved to Jenna and Dennis, who were working their way toward them through the crowd. It was so sweet, the way they wrapped their arms around each other. Jenna had her head on Dennis's shoulder and they looked like they had eyes only for each other, in spite of the crowd around them. "What happened to the big night out at the bar?"

"We might have figured out another name for our suspect list," Jenna offered as she took a step away from Dennis. "Corbin Wells. His sister Wendy works at the Inn. He'd had a few drinks in him, but he was spouting off to anyone who would listen that Travis was a no-good SOB who'd gotten what he deserved."

"I started up a conversation with one of the other guys, who confirmed that Corbin has been on a manhunt ever since he found out that his sister was forced to engage in acts he didn't want to discuss after agreeing to have a drink with Travis at the end of her shift."

"It sounds like he might be our guy," Tj agreed.

"Where are the girls?" Jenna asked.

"Your mom took them home," Tj answered.

"Did you ever get a chance to talk to Sean?"

"Dylan did," Tj told Jenna. "He claims to have been at the resort during the time Travis was killed, but he doesn't remember seeing anyone who could corroborate his story."

"You don't think he's a serious suspect?" Dennis asked.

"Not really. We added him to the list because Travis's death will benefit his career, but he doesn't seem the type to be a murderer. Still, I'd like to confirm an alibi so I can cross him off."

"Who's left?" Jenna asked.

Tj took out her phone and considered her notes. "Pete Quinn is my top suspect at this point. Dylan found out that he was blackmailing Travis over a steroid cover-up. Travis burned down the evidence, so it makes sense that Pete might have been upset that the gravy train had come to an end. If you add the fact that Travis basically bilked him out of a lot of money when he promised to sign with him as a sponsor and then didn't, it seems he has a pretty good motive."

"Have you talked to him?" Dennis wondered.

"Not yet. I checked at his shop and the staff said he was in Sacramento for a few days. It seems odd that he'd be gone at such a busy time, but I suppose it's possible. Until I can verify that, he stays at the top of the list."

"Who else?" Jenna asked.

"Mayor Wallaby and Johnson claim to have been together, but according to Harriet the timing is off. And according to Dylan, they had plenty of time to have the argument they told Dylan about and then return to the mountain and kill Travis. Johnson said he went home after talking to Wallaby. Unfortunately, he was alone. Dylan has Roy and Tim talking to neighbors. Wallaby won't tell Dylan where he went after arguing with Johnson."

"He was most likely with a woman," Dennis said.

"That was my guess as well," Tj confirmed.

"Okay, so we have Pete, Wallaby, Johnson, and Sean with unconfirmed alibis," Jenna summarized. "Anyone else?"

"Albert Pitman confessed to drugging Travis but claims he didn't kill him. While that may be true, it could also be a ploy, so he stays on the list."

"Don't forget to add Corbin," Jenna reminded her.

"I will. And Wendy as well. Doc mentioned that she was supposed to be a judge at the chowder cook-off today but didn't show."

"I thought our plan was to make a list and whittle it down, but it seems like it keeps getting longer," Jenna pointed out.

"Travis was a toad. There are a lot of people in town with motives," Tj answered.

CHAPTER 17

Saturday, February 22

Tj woke early the following morning. She was going to have a full day at the carnival, but she decided she wasn't going anywhere until she tracked down the missing pet. Yesterday morning she'd done a cursory search, but she hadn't been overly worried at that point, so she really hadn't looked beyond the surface. When she'd gotten home last night, the girls had been asleep, and she hadn't wanted to wake them, so she'd looked around but hadn't really torn the place apart. This morning, if their furry gray friend didn't make an appearance, she'd dismantle the house board by board if she had to.

"Any sign of Crissy?" Tj asked Ben, who was making coffee.

"Not yet."

"Gracie still sleeping?" Tj poured a large mug of the hot liquid.

"Yeah. She had trouble falling asleep, so she's probably pretty tired."

"You know this house better than anyone," Tj said. Ben had built the house from logs he'd milled himself. "Where could she be hiding?"

Ben thought about it. "We know that Gracie took Crissy to

bed with her on Thursday night. She was gone Friday morning. The only way she could have gotten out is if someone had gone in and left the door open."

"I went in to kiss her good night when I got home," Tj confirmed. "I don't remember seeing Crissy, but the door was open for about a minute while I tucked her blankets around her and kissed her forehead."

"Has she ever tried to get out before when you've gone in to say good night?"

"No. Most of the time she's sleeping right there on the bed."

"But she wasn't there that night?"

Tj thought about it. "I'm not sure. It was late, and Gracie was already asleep. I left the hall light on but didn't turn on the light in the bedroom. I was tired, so it was a quick kiss, but I honestly don't remember if Crissy was there or not."

"Seems odd that she'd take off that way." Ben shook his head.

"Not if she's sick. Animals do that," Tj worried aloud. "They go off alone to die."

"Did you check the attic?" Ben asked.

"The attic?"

"When the power went out during last week's storm, I went up into the attic to get some more blankets for the girls' beds. I suppose it's possible I didn't close the door tightly."

"It's worth a try." Tj hurried to the pull-down stairs that led to the attic. The stairs were pulled up and the latch was fastened tightly, so Crissy couldn't have squeezed through. Still, as long as she was here, it was worth taking a look. She'd pretty much looked everywhere else. She pulled down the stairs and climbed them one by one until she reached the large room, which covered the living space below.

"Crissy," she called. "Are you in here, sweetie?"

Tj let out a happy breath when she heard a faint cry. It sounded like it was coming from the area directly above Gracie's room. There was a ceiling access to the attic from there, so maybe Crissy had worked it free and climbed inside.

The attic was stacked from floor to ceiling with old furniture and storage boxes. Her dad and grandfather both tended to be pack rats who were reluctant to throw things away. As Tj maneuvered around the debris accumulated over three generations, she continued to call the missing cat.

"Crissy?" Tj stopped near a pile of old clothes. "Well, I'll be."

Crissy was stretched out on her grandpa's old winter coat. Beside her were two kittens, one white and one black. Tj should have recognized the signs, but she'd been so busy she'd barely paid any attention at all to the cat, who was mostly cared for by Gracie.

"You've picked yourself a nice spot to have your babies, but it's kind of cold up here. Maybe you'd like to move downstairs?"

Crissy began to purr.

Tj found an empty box and lined it with an old but soft blanket. Carefully transferring the kittens inside, she called to Crissy and started back down the stairs. Closing the access firmly behind her, she carried the box into Gracie's room. Crissy and her babies would be comfortable in Gracie's closet, away from the hustle and bustle of the main living area. Tj knew it wouldn't be long before Crissy would leave her babies for a short time each day, but for now she'd set up a feeding station and litter box close by.

"Look what I found." Tj kissed Gracie on the head to wake her up.

"Crissy," she yelled as she hugged the cat. "Where did you go? I was so sad without you."

"I think she was busy." Tj set the box on the floor next to the bed so Gracie could see the kittens.

"She made babies?"

"Looks like."

"Can we keep them?"

"We'll see. For now, let's get the new family settled in your closet."

"Can I hold one?"

"Not yet." Tj sat down next to Gracie. "This is very important, so I want you to listen carefully."

"'Kay."

"Crissy's babies are too little to hold. If you pick them up, you might hurt them. I'm going to let them stay in here with you, but you have to promise not to touch them until I say it's okay. Deal?"

"Deal." Gracie grinned.

Tj had a full morning of events. She wanted to fill Dylan in on Corbin Wells's outburst the previous evening, but she knew she wouldn't have time to meet him until the afternoon. She texted him and asked if he'd be free to meet her for lunch. He texted back to say he'd love to meet her if they could do it at one thirty. She confirmed the time and asked him to meet her in front of Grainger's General Store.

Mike informed the family that he would be tied up with events at the resort all day so they shouldn't include him in any plans they might make. Grandpa likewise reported that he, along with Doc and Bookman, were going to take all four girls to the ice-sculpting competition, since Helen, Bonnie, and Jenna were going to be busy at the Antiquery until after three. Gracie hadn't wanted to go at first because she felt it was her duty to stay home to take care of her new family, but Tj had convinced her that babies needed lots of rest during the first few days of their lives and it was best to let Crissy have some peace and quiet. Gracie was reluctant until Mike promised he'd stop in to check on them every now and then.

"I didn't expect to see you today," Jenna commented as Tj poured herself a cup of coffee, snagged a couple of cookies off the cooling rack, and slid onto one of the stools lining the counter.

"I'm taking Dylan to lunch as an apology for not trusting him with the whole Josh situation. I thought I'd stop by to pick something up and then take him on a picnic."

"Isn't it a little cold to be sitting on the ground?" Jenna slid the sandwich she was grilling onto a plate.

"We're not having our picnic on the ground; we're having it in the sleigh. I want to take Dylan up to Pine Nut Hill to watch the ice skating in the cove."

"Sounds romantic." Jenna smiled as she scooped potato salad onto a plate next to a sandwich and rang the bell for her sister Bren to pick up the order.

"It does," Tj agreed. "However, my plan, for the short time I have his undivided attention, is to talk murder, so I'm not sure how romantic it will actually be."

"Maybe you should give the investigation a break and focus on the beautiful sunny day, the romantic horse-drawn sleigh, the handsome man next to you, and the delicious lunch I'm about to prepare for you," Jenna said.

"Maybe you're right."

"Dennis heard from Josh," Jenna informed her. "His dad is doing better, and they think they can save his arm. Josh hasn't told him about Travis yet, which he thinks he'll take hard. They weren't really close—in fact, Travis hated him quite a lot—but I guess Bert hadn't given up hope of establishing relationships with both of his sons."

"Poor guy," Tj sympathized.

"Josh is coming back to work on Monday. Bert will have to stay in Sacramento for a while, but Josh figures he can visit on his days off."

"Has he told his mom what's going on?" Tj wondered.

Jenna nodded. "She took it better than he expected. He doubts they'll ever be one big happy family, but he said she seemed fine with him pursuing the relationship. By the way, before I forget to mention it, Dolly was in again today. And, as expected, Sean was in as well. He was sitting at a table with his coach and Dolly was sitting alone across the room. They didn't speak or make eye contact, but they arrived at about the same time and left within minutes of each other."

"Sean has to notice that this woman is following him around," Tj speculated.

"I'm sure he must. The only thing I can come up with is that Dolly is some kind of bodyguard."

Tj laughed. "Have you seen her? She weighs like a hundred pounds. I doubt she'd be much help in a scuffle."

"Yeah, you're right. Maybe you should just ask Sean what's up. By the way," Jenna smiled a secret little smile that let Tj know she was up to something, "be sure to be at the auditorium by three."

"Something going on?"

"It's a surprise."

*   *   *

"When you suggested lunch, I had no idea you were planning something so special," Dylan commented as the sleigh glided through the silent forest toward the cove where the ice skating was being held. "What's the occasion?"

"No occasion." Tj leaned her head against Dylan's shoulder. He had insisted on driving when he found out the mode of transportation they'd be taking. Normally, Tj didn't have a lot of patience with guys who had the need to be all macho, but she owed Dylan, and if he wanted to drive, she'd let him. Besides, it was nice to snuggle up next to him under the blanket she'd brought and let him do all the work. "I just wanted to apologize for the whole thing with Josh. I need you to know that I really do feel bad."

"Am I to assume you cooked for this occasion?"

Tj laughed. "I'm happy to inform you that Jenna cooked. She's sorry too."

Dylan found a flat spot overlooking the cove and brought the sleigh to a stop. Tj provided the horses with a snack while Dylan dug into the basket Jenna had packed.

"This soup is really good." Dylan shoveled a spoonful into his mouth.

"Jenna is a really good cook, and soup is one of her specialties."

"It's really beautiful up here," Dylan added. "So quiet and peaceful. It's really nice after the long week I've had."

Tj broke off a corner of the bread Jenna had packed and began nibbling on one end. "Are you working tonight? Jenna's sister Bren is participating in the ice princess competition, so I plan to attend. It would be fun to go together."

"If nothing comes up, I should be off by five," Dylan said.

"Tim and Roy are tracking down a couple of leads, so you never know what could happen."

"Speaking of leads..." Tj began.

"I wondered how long it would take for you to come around to the real reason for this lunch." Dylan grinned.

"The real reason for this lunch was an apology," Tj insisted. "If you don't want to know what I found out, I don't have to tell you."

"I was just kidding." Dylan smiled. "Hit me with your news."

"I have a couple of new suspects," Tj began. "I don't know if they'll pan out, but I wanted to make sure you knew everything I know."

"I appreciate that." Dylan dipped a piece of his bread into his thick creamy broth. "So what do you have for me?"

"I remembered Chelsea's boyfriend had been in a fistfight with Travis prior to his death. I don't think this would put him really high on our list, but he should be added all the same."

"Duly noted," Dylan teased. "But the boyfriend isn't our guy. I've already talked to him and he has an alibi. What else do you have for me?"

"Corbin Wells. Dennis and Jenna overheard him say that Travis was a no-good SOB who'd gotten what he deserved. It seems that Corbin has been on a manhunt ever since he found out that his sister was forced to engage in acts he didn't want to discuss after she agreed to drinks with Trevor at the end of her shift. I remember Chelsea saying that Sarah wasn't the first girl Travis had sexually abused. Wendy works at the Inn, so I'm thinking he might be our guy."

"It sounds like someone we should definitely follow up on," Dylan agreed.

It had begun to snow lightly, making Tj wish more than

ever that they were there to discuss something other than murder.

The setting begged for romance, but all Tj had been able to come up with were suspects and alibis. Maybe Jenna was right; maybe she did need to have her head examined.

"I was hesitant to bring this up at first, but I think you should also talk to Wendy Wells. Wendy is sort of shy, and if Travis did rape her, she isn't likely to want to talk about it. I think it will be important to treat her with kid gloves, and let her set the pace of the conversation."

"I'll keep that in mind," Dylan promised. "I'm not an ogre, you know."

"I know. It's just that Sheriff Boggs can be a curmudgeon, and since he's heading the investigation, folks are being careful. You're new, and people don't really know you yet. Once you're here for a while, I think you'll find people to be a little more cooperative."

"Including a certain auburn-haired high-school coach?" Dylan looked Tj directly in the eye and leaned in close, as if he might kiss her.

"Especially a certain auburn-haired high-school coach," Tj whispered as she tilted her head toward his.

Dylan was inches from her mouth when his phone started to ring. He took it out of his pocket and looked at the caller ID. "I need to get this. Hey, sis," he said with a smile.

Tj watched as his smile faded. "What happened?" he asked.

Tj sat quietly as Dylan frowned at whatever his sister was telling him. She figured it must be hard on him to be so far away from his family after having been so much a part of their lives. Before Ashley and Gracie had come to live with them, she couldn't imagine wanting kids, but now...now she couldn't imagine life without them.

"Okay, put him on." Dylan sighed. "Hey, buddy. Your mom tells me that you've been having some trouble at school."

Tj watched Dylan's expression change as he listened to whatever story his nephew was telling him. Tj knew that after Dylan's sister Allie had become pregnant with his eight-year-old nephew Justin, her boyfriend had deserted her, and Dylan had helped her raise the boy. Then, when Dylan's wife was murdered during a shootout in which he'd been the intended victim, Allie had become concerned about Justin's safety while he was with his uncle, refusing to let the boy visit him. Once Dylan had recovered from the extensive wounds he'd received in the shootout, he'd moved to Serenity from Chicago. He hadn't seen Justin since the incident, although they spoke by phone regularly.

"I know. I miss you too." Dylan rubbed his forehead with his free hand. "I understand what you're saying, but your mom is really worried about you. Maybe we can work something else out. I'll tell you what: I want you to get caught up with all your homework and I'll talk to your mom about letting you visit over the summer."

Dylan smiled at something Justin said. "Okay, but remember, nothing less than your best behavior." He glanced at Tj and smiled. "Okay, I promise, now put your mom back on."

Tj tried not to listen as Dylan spoke to his sister about what was obviously a private family matter, but it was sort of hard not to hear when she was sitting shoulder to shoulder with the man. By the sound of things, Justin had decided not only to boycott his schoolwork until his mom agreed to let him visit his uncle but he'd been acting out as well.

Based on Dylan's side of the conversation, Allie was at the end of her rope. Dylan was treating her with love and patience, which made Tj respect him more than she already did. She couldn't imagine how hard the entire situation must be for him.

"Sorry about that," he said after he hung up. "Justin is having some problems in school."

"I gathered," Tj replied. "I've been having some problems with Ashley as well."

Tj explained about Ashley's outburst over not being invited to Loretta Baldwin's party and the backlash that had resulted from the fight she'd initiated.

She filled him in on the history of Ashley's relationship with Loretta, and the fact that she was just as happy that Ashley wasn't friends with the mean child, though she did understand how difficult it must be to be an outcast at a new school where she'd been trying so hard to fit in.

"What Ashley needs is a generalized elevation of status," Dylan responded. "She's had a tough year, and it's never easy to start off at a new school. To make matters worse, she made an enemy of a very influential class member. If she can notch up her position on the overall popularity scale a bit and provide a circumstance for her to show that she's the bigger person, it'll be harder for kids like Loretta to pick on her."

"That actually makes sense." Tj was impressed. "Any idea how to accomplish that?"

Dylan thought about it. "I'm doing a safety assembly at the school next week. I'll ask Ashley to be my special assistant. During the demonstration, I'll ask her to pick a classmate to help out as well. Experience has shown that all the kids will want to do it. We'll instruct Ashley to pick Loretta."

"Loretta?" Tj asked. "After everything she's done to Ashley?"

"The problem with Loretta started when Ashley first started school after the death of her mother. No one can blame her for pushing Loretta after what she said, but it appears Loretta has managed to spin the situation her own way, making Ashley look like the bad guy. If she picks Loretta to help out with the assembly, it will serve as an apology of sorts, thereby ending the feud. If Loretta continues to pick on her, my guess is that the other kids will side with Ashley."

"We'll have to fill Kristi in on the plan or her feelings will be hurt if Ashley doesn't pick her."

"I'm sure she'll understand."

"You're pretty good at this parenting thing," Tj complimented.

Dylan sighed. "When it comes to other people's kids. I'm afraid I may have made a horrible mistake with Justin."

"How so?"

"I'm the only dad Justin has ever known. I never should have left him behind to come to Serenity."

"But I thought you told me your sister wouldn't let you see him after your wife was killed."

"Yeah, she was afraid that if he'd been at our apartment, as he often was, he might have been killed as well. I don't blame her for being scared. But Justin needs to have me in his life, and if I'd stayed, I could have convinced her of that eventually. When I left Chicago, I tried to tell myself that taking this job was the best thing for everyone, but I can see now that what I was really doing was running away from a situation that had become too intense for me to handle."

"Are you thinking about going back?" Tj's heart sank.

"I don't know. Maybe. If I can't convince Allie to move out here."

Tj didn't want to think about Dylan leaving, but she knew that once you gave your heart to a child, they owned it. If Ashley and Gracie's happiness depended on her moving to be with them, she knew she'd do it in a minute.

CHAPTER 18

"Coach Jensen," Sarah, who had been talking with Brittany and Jilli, called as she raced across the parking lot of the auditorium, where Tj was supposed to meet Jenna. Tj started to wave as Sarah caught up to her and wrapped her in a hug so tight Tj could barely breathe. Tj hugged her back. "Thank you," Sarah whispered into her ear. "Really." She pulled back enough to look Tj directly in the eye. "Thank you."

"You're doing good?" Tj asked as Sarah took a small step back.

"I am." Sarah released her grip so that they stood face to face. "Better than good. I had my first counseling session on Thursday. In one session, my counselor's already helped me see how totally out of balance my life has been since my dad died, my sister went off to college and the majority of the responsibility of raising my brother and sisters has fallen on me. It's a complicated situation, because my mom really does have to work, but Mom is joining me for my Tuesday session, and we're going to work on a strategy that will work for everyone."

"That's wonderful, Sarah."

"And Brittany and Jilli have been great," she added. "They told me how much you helped them when Jilli's dad died and Brittany's parents decided to get divorced. We all think you're a great coach, but maybe your true calling is as a counselor or something."

Tj grinned. "Thanks, but I think I'll stick to coaching."

"Yeah, sports at school would suck without you."

"Have you talked to Eric?" Tj wondered.

"Yeah. A lot, actually. He's hurt, but he loves me and wants to work on our relationship. As friends for now, but maybe someday..."

"Has he started counseling as well?"

"Next week. On Monday. I think he's seeing someone Principal Remington recommended to his parents."

"I'm glad everything worked out."

"Me too." Sarah hugged Tj again. "I should get back, but I just wanted to say thanks."

Tj watched as Sarah trotted back toward Brittany and Jilli. She was glad everything had turned out well. Being a teenager was hard; a lot of adults forgot how hard. Tj might have lost points on her evaluation for being too much of a friend to her students, but in the end, she'd take the ding on her review if it meant her students felt comfortable confiding in her when they needed help.

"That Sarah?" Ben walked up behind her.

"Yeah." Tj watched as Sarah looped her arm through Jilli's as they continued toward the auditorium.

"How's she doing?"

"Better. So what's the big secret?"

"The ice princess pageant."

"Oh God. You didn't enter me, did you?"

"No." Ben chuckled. "As you already pointed out, you're much too old. Today's competition is the junior princess category. The minimum age to enter is eight, so Ashley and Kristi decided to give it a try."

Tj and Ben walked together toward the building. "I'm going to go out on a limb here and guess that Helen is the one who talked the girls into doing this."

"Good guess," Ben said with a laugh.

"Does Ashley have a dress?" Tj was certain she didn't have one, if the decision to enter the contest was little more than a whim.

"Helen took the girls shopping and bought them both new dresses. And she took them for manicures and haircuts as well."

"I thought Helen was working today." Tj hadn't actually seen her at the Antiquery when she'd been there earlier, but she'd made the assumption she was in the front, where the antiques were displayed and sold.

"Bonnie covered for her."

"I can't believe Ashley is doing this," Tj commented. "Was Gracie jealous?"

"No. The boys and I took the two younger girls out to lunch and then to a movie. Jenna brought them special 'little sister' corsages for their wrists. They seem pretty happy."

"Is Jenna here?" Tj asked. Normally, the café didn't even close until three.

"They closed early. She's with the girls and Helen in the back. Dennis is around somewhere. He has his camera and is taking photos."

"And Dad?"

"He's already inside with the others. They're saving us seats."

Tj looked around as they entered the crowded auditorium. She hoped Ashley didn't suffer from a case of stage fright at the last minute.

Of course, she'd been taking dance classes for a while, and she'd recently signed up for community theater, and she wasn't really shy. Tj began to relax as she realized her sister would most likely do just fine.

"Good, you made it." Mike lifted his jacket off the seat he'd been saving for her. "They're about to start."

Twenty-seven girls between the ages of eight and eleven walked in single file onto the stage. Each was wearing a beautiful dress and had elegantly styled hair. They really did look like little princesses, Tj thought. Ashley waved as she took her place on the stage. Helen had done a good job picking out the perfect dress to go with her light red hair, which was styled into a twist on the top of her head. She looked beautiful, and happy, and mature. Tj frowned. The little girl she'd come to know over the past six months was gone, and in her place was the hint of the beautiful young woman she would become. Tj was surprised to find she wasn't quite ready for Ashley to grow up. When the sisters had first come to live with her, she hadn't known what she was going to do with two little girls. Now she didn't know what she'd do without them.

"She looks so old," Mike commented.

"I was thinking the same thing," Tj whispered back.

"Is she wearing makeup?"

"I think so."

"She looks beautiful, but I'm not sure I'm ready for this."

"Preaching to the choir." Tj leaned her head on her dad's shoulder. She remembered how he'd resisted her growing up. Each milestone had been accompanied by a sad discourse about how his little girl was no longer his little girl. At the time, Tj had rolled her eyes in disgust, but sitting in the crowded auditorium, watching her own little girl take her first step toward womanhood, she knew exactly how he'd felt.

"Kristi looks nice too," Mike offered.

"I love her dress." Helen had picked a royal-blue velvet that looked lovely with Kristi's long blond hair and bright blue eyes.

"Shhh. Ashley's next for her speech." Mike beamed like a proud grandpa.

Each girl was asked why she wanted to be the junior ice princess, and what her talent would be. Ashley said that she didn't really want to be an ice princess but preferred to be an ice queen, since queens had more power and got more respect than princesses. This had everyone laughing, which she didn't seem to mind. She announced that her talent would be to sing a song.

Kristi announced that she wanted to be princess so she could ride on the float during the Kick Off to Summer Parade, which was held in June. And her talent was going to be to dance her favorite ballet.

By the time the girls began to come out for the talent portion of the competition, Tj's stomach was in knots. After years of coaching the area's youth and dealing with anxious and opinionated parents, Tj had sworn that if she ever had kids of her own, she wouldn't stress over every little thing. Yet here she was with butterflies in her stomach as she worried about whether Ashley knew a song, and if she'd sing off-key, and if she'd be mortified if she messed up or tripped as she walked onto the stage.

"I'm so nervous," Tj confessed. "How do parents do this day after day?"

"You get used to it," Mike promised. Ashley began the long walk onto the stage when it was her turn. "Or not." Tj noticed he was holding his breath as she made her way up the stairs in her new shoes.

Tj laced her fingers through her dad's as they both forgot to breathe as the stage lights dimmed. Ashley looked confident and happy as she began to sing a ballad Tj had no idea she'd ever even heard.

"She's good." Tj let out her breath.

"Thank God." Mike let his out as well.

"Who would have thought?" Tj was stunned.

"Our baby is going to be a star."

In the end, Ashley and Kristi both were fantastic, but neither girl placed, which wasn't surprising; almost every year, the princess and her court were eleven-year-olds competing for the last time before moving up to the twelve- to fifteen-year-old category.

"That was fun." Ashley bounded up and hugged her sister. "Can we stay and watch Aunt Bren?"

"The girls sixteen to twenty-one won't get started for a couple of hours. How about some dinner?" Tj suggested.

"Can we get tacos?" Ashley asked.

Tj glanced at Jenna, who had just walked up with Kristi.

"Tacos are good," she agreed.

"We'll need a table for thirteen," Tj calculated.

"Helen, Bonnie, and the boys and I," Ben said, referring to Doc and Bookman, "are going to head over to Murphy's for a cold one."

"Okay, make that eight."

"I think I'm going to see how Rosalie is doing," Mike added.

"We're down to seven. I assume Dennis is coming with us?"

"He ran into Josh. I told him I'd just meet him back here for Bren's pageant," Jenna informed her.

"Okay, six it is. Beach Hut Taco okay?'

"Sounds good," Jenna agreed.

Beach Hut Taco was a taqueria on the edge of town. A bit nicer than fast food, the menu was simple and inexpensive. After ordering their meals, Tj and Jenna settled down with their blended margaritas while the girls played video games.

"So Gracie tells me you have two new members of the family," Jenna began.

"We do," Tj confirmed. "A black kitten named Midnight and a white one named Snowy."

"Uh-oh." Jenna grimaced. "You've named them. You know once you name them, you'll never be able to give them away."

"I figured. At first I thought the last thing we needed were two more mouths to feed, but let's face it, the house is a zoo already. What are two more residents? Once the babies get older, Ashley wants to have Snowy sleep in her room, and Grandpa said he'd take Midnight."

"Really?"

"I was surprised too, but he said it'd be nice to have a warm body to cuddle up with after all these years."

"I guess I understand that." Jenna smiled.

"Yeah, Cuervo's a grouch and Echo is a pillow hog, but I don't know what I'd do if I didn't have them to come home to every night."

"Not much room left for a man," Jenna teased.

"Who needs a man when you have a cat that snores and a dog that sleeps in the middle of the bed?" Tj laughed.

"Speaking of men, tell me about your lunch," Jenna encouraged.

"It was nice." Tj took a sip of her drink. "We mostly talked suspects and alibis, but it was cozy and romantic and, most importantly, I think we cleared the air about a few things. He got an upsetting call from his sister that ended things on a sour note, but I've decided I'm not going to worry about that right now. He texted and said he needed to work late, but he's going to meet us at the auditorium at eight for Bren's pageant."

"I'm sure Mom and Bonnie will come back to watch Bren, but I doubt we'll see your grandpa and his posse again."

"I think one princess pageant a day is their limit. You mentioned that Dennis ran into Josh. How's he doing?"

"Dennis says okay. It seems Travis's death hit him hard. The guy was a jerk, but he was his brother. His dad is doing better. If nothing else, I think this whole thing brought them closer together."

"That's good." Tj watched as Sean Wright walked past the restaurant on the sidewalk outside, Dolly following right behind him. There was no way Sean didn't notice her.

"Dennis said Josh is going to see to Travis's funeral once the investigation is complete. His mom is in rehab and isn't really able to deal with things. According to Dennis, the woman has OD'd so many times she's barely coherent."

"That's nice."

"Are you even listening to me?" Jenna asked.

Tj looked away from the window. "Sorry. I saw Sean walk by with Dolly less than twenty feet behind him and I got distracted."

"That whole thing is really odd," Jenna said. "I guess you can just ask one or both of them what's going on."

"Yeah, I've thought about it. Not that it's any of my business, but I have to admit the situation has me intrigued. It's almost like the woman is tailing him, but she's being so obvious about it that you'd think Sean would tell her to get lost."

"I know I would," Jenna said. "It looks like our order is up. I'll get the girls."

CHAPTER 19

When Tj and Jenna got back to the auditorium, Dylan and Dennis were waiting outside. Tj groaned when she noticed that the line to get in was twice as long as it had been earlier in the day.

"Wow, what a huge turnout," Jenna commented after kissing her husband. "We're never going to get seats."

"Our mothers are already inside," Dennis informed her. "They saved seats, but they want us to hurry. They've already had a handful of people argue that saving seats isn't allowed when there's a full house."

"Okay," Jenna said, grabbing Kari's hand. "Let's go."

"We'll take the girls inside," Dennis offered. "Dylan has something to discuss with Tj. We're near the front, about five rows up from the stage. Saving two seats with eight people should be easier than saving eight seats with two people, but you still might want to hurry."

"We will," Tj promised. "What's up?" she asked the handsome deputy, who was dressed in dark brown cords and a forest green and tan sweater rather than his uniform.

Dylan took a hand-drawn sketch from his pocket. "Do you recognize this woman?"

Tj bit her lip as she scrutinized the portrait. She didn't think the woman was anyone she knew, although she looked oddly familiar. Based on her slim face and delicate bone structure, Tj bet she had a petite frame. She had almond-shaped eyes and long black hair that hung to the middle of her back. After running a mental scan of all of the women she knew who fit this basic description, no one came to mind.

"She looks sort of familiar, but I don't think I know her. Why?"

"This is the sketch artist's depiction of a woman one of the maids at the Inn saw in the hall near Travis's room the night he was killed. The maid admits to only glancing at her as she walked by."

"Chances are the likeness isn't even close," Tj guessed.

"Yeah, the odds of it being close enough for anyone to recognize are slim, but it was worth a try. You were in the bar an hour before Travis was killed. Do you remember anyone with a yellow jacket and dark hair?"

Tj thought about it. "No, sorry. At least not specifically. I'm sure there were a lot of people with dark hair, but I'm pretty sure I didn't see anyone with a yellow jacket. Can I keep the drawing?"

"Yeah, I have copies."

Tj folded the portrait and put it in her pocket. "Did you have a chance to talk to Corbin?"

Dylan nodded. "He says he was drunk when he was spouting off at the bar and doesn't remember what he said. He claims he was most likely just showing off, because as far as he knows, his sister has never even met Travis."

"Does he have an alibi?"

"A weak one. He said he was at a nightclub on the strip in Indulgence. I checked with the owner, who verified that Corbin's a regular, but he can't swear he was there that night. He's going to check credit-card receipts and get back to me."

"Do you think Corbin lied?" Tj wondered.

"Honestly, no. He must know I'll check his alibi. If he wasn't at the club, why say he was? He would have been better off telling me he was alone than giving an alibi that won't check out. Still, he stays on the list until I talk to the nightclub owner again tomorrow."

"And Wendy?" Tj wondered.

"I went by her apartment, but she wasn't home. Tim said he knows her pretty well, so he's going to track her down and have a talk with her."

"Anything else?"

"I found out that Pete Quinn made a call to the Inn on Sunday evening, demanding to talk to Travis. My guess is that he heard about the fire and was outraged."

"Sounds like a motive to me," Tj replied. "Whatever happened with his alibi?"

"He said he went for a bike ride along the American River Bike Trail in Sacramento because the roads up here are covered with snow. Unfortunately, he went alone, and he claims he paid cash for everything, so he doesn't have any receipts or any other proof to show he was there."

"Sounds fishy to me," Tj said. "Although, if it helps, I know he's a serious road biker. Let's go in. The pageant is going to start any minute."

"Tj..."

"Yeah?"

"There's one more thing. You're not going to like this, but I had to add Hunter to the list of suspects."

"What?" Tj was certain she'd misunderstood. "Why would you suspect Hunter?"

"When I was up at Angel Mountain talking to Pete Quinn, he mentioned he'd seen Hunter there on the day Travis was killed. He said it was earlier in the day—at least several hours before Chelsea came bursting into the bar—but he thought he'd mention it all the same."

"Why would he do that?" Tj wondered.

"He's one of the prime suspects in this case. His alibi can't be confirmed, and Josh has already suggested that he's guilty of blackmail. He needed to give me something. It's a ploy I've seen time and time again; suspects often attempt to divert the attention away from themselves."

"So he threw Hunter under the bus," Tj supposed.

"Basically. At first I wasn't too worried about it, but I called Hunter and explained what I had heard and why I needed his alibi."

"And?"

"Hunter verified that he'd been at Angel Mountain and that he'd argued with Travis. I guess Travis had been giving Chelsea a bad time and Hunter wanted to communicate to him that if he valued his health, he'd best back off of hassling his sister."

"I'm sure it was just a figure of speech," Tj defended. "Hunter would never hurt anyone."

"I agree."

"So why put him on the list?"

"It's my job to put everyone on the list who has motive and opportunity and doesn't have an alibi."

"Hunter doesn't have an alibi?" Tj paled.

"According to the staff at the hospital, Hunter took an early lunch but promised to be back for his afternoon appointments. Two hours later, he called his nurse, told her something had come up, and asked her to clear his day. Hunter admitted that after his discussion with Travis he'd been too worked up to see patients, so he got in his car and took a long drive. He doesn't remember seeing anyone who could vouch for his whereabouts between noon and nine o'clock, when he got home."

Dylan put his hands on Tj's upper arms. "I don't believe Hunter did this any more than you do, but I wouldn't be doing my job if I didn't put him on the list. Tomorrow I'm going to work on finding someone who saw him after he left the resort, but I wanted you to hear this from me now, in case someone said something to you about it tonight."

"What if he doesn't have an alibi?" she asked.

"Then he'll be cleared when we find the real killer," he assured her. "Okay?" Dylan bent his head so he was looking her in the eye.

Tj looked back at him. "Okay."

By the time Tj got home, she was physically and mentally exhausted. Her dad helped her to carry the girls up to bed. Crissy, Midnight, and Snowy were asleep on Gracie's bed. The silly cat must have moved her babies from the closet to the bed while they were gone. Gracie was small and she had a big bed, and in spite of what Ashley said, she was actually a very quiet sleeper. Tj thought about moving the cat family back to the box in the closet but decided to trust Crissy's mothering instinct and let her decide where she wanted to sleep. If she wanted her babies back in the box, Tj supposed she could move them there the same way she'd gotten them from the box to the bed in the first place.

Echo was thrilled to have Tj home. It had been a busy couple of weeks and he hadn't gotten his usual amount of mom-and-dog time. Grabbing her snowshoes and pulling on a heavy coat, Tj slipped a hat onto her head and mittens onto her hands and went back out into the cold night air. Echo romped along beside her as she walked down the path to the lake. In spite of the frigid temperature, it really was a beautiful night. The moon was bright, the sky was clear, and the air was perfectly still. The dog picked up a stick and ran down the snow-covered beach as Tj followed behind. She couldn't imagine living in a city where a late-night stroll would take place on a busy street with the smell of exhaust and the sound of traffic as the backdrop. She paused and closed her eyes, letting her senses take over as she felt her stress dissolve. The only sound she heard was panting as Echo sat down by her side.

Tj tried to focus on the serenity around her. She wasn't going to be able to help Hunter or anyone else if she drove herself crazy. She took a deep breath and focused on the scents around her. During the summer, fires from the campground filled the air with a smoky aroma that brought back fond memories of camping with her dad. Tonight, however, the only fragrance that permeated the night air was the smell of something wonderful coming from the Lakeside Bar and Grill, which served appetizers until two a.m. on Saturday nights.

Calling Echo to her side, Tj changed direction. She'd poke her head in the kitchen to see if whoever was working that night would make her an order of chili fries to go. Luckily, the night chef, Jason, was in the kitchen, so she was able to put in her order from the back door.

"Why didn't you call over?" Jason asked. "I would have had it ready for you when you got here."

"I was out for a walk and had a craving," Tj explained as she slipped off her snowshoes and leaned them against the wall outside the door.

"I heard your downhill team dominated at the carnival events."

"First place," Tj bragged.

"Want me to bag up something for Echo?" Jason asked. Tj had left Echo waiting obediently outside the kitchen door, but his adorable face could be seen looking in through the nearby window.

"Yeah, he deserves a treat. Is the bar busy tonight?"

"Most of the guests have left. Sean Wright and his coach are finishing up a beer."

"And Dolly?" Tj asked. Anyone who'd been around during the past ten days knew exactly who she was referring to.

"I haven't seen her all day."

"Does she ever talk to anyone when she's here?" Tj asked.

"Nope. Just sits with her book. Although I don't think she's actually reading."

"Why do you say that?"

"I was working the bar the other night. It was slow, so I was watching her out of the corner of my eye. In the hour she was here, I never saw her turn a page."

"And Sean was here as well?"

"Table in the corner, where he's spent almost every night since he's been here," Jason confirmed. "Your order's ready. Want some ranch dressing for dipping?"

Tj quietly wound her way along the walkway that connected the cabins. The beach was a more direct route to the main house, but she'd already cleared the snow from her snowshoes and didn't want to have to repeat the exercise. As she passed Sean's cabin, she paused. There was definitely someone inside. She'd noticed that Sean was still in the bar when she'd left the restaurant and wondered who it could be. As far as she knew, he was staying alone.

She paused and looked in the front window. Inside was a young girl sitting in a recliner, watching television. The girl was petite, with a slight frame and long dark hair. It was hard to tell from her vantage point, but if Tj didn't know better, she'd swear the girl looked remarkably like the one in Dylan's sketch. Tj made a split-second decision and jogged to the lodge. She left her snowshoes, fries, and Echo with the desk clerk and grabbed a handful of towels. Returning to the cabin, she knocked. She looked in through the window as the girl looked around frantically. Tj knocked on the window to let the girl know that she'd seen her. The girl hesitated, then walked toward the door.

"Can I help you?" She opened the door a few inches and peeked out.

"I brought the towels you requested."

"I'm sorry, you must have the wrong cabin. I didn't ask for any towels."

Tj frowned, intentionally conveying a look of confusion. She took a blank piece of paper out of her pocket and pretended to be studying it. "This is Sean Wright's cabin?"

"Y-yes," the girl stammered.

"That's odd. The desk clerk specifically asked me to drop these towels at Sean Wright's cabin."

The girl opened the door wider. "I'll take them."

Tj tried not to gasp when she noticed the yellow jacket on the coat rack inside. "It says here," she pretended to consult the fake information sheet, "that Sean Wright is staying alone."

"I'm his cousin, Serena," the girl explained. "I'm in town on a project. Sean said it would be okay if I stayed with him. It's a big cabin," she pointed out.

"I'm sure that's fine," Tj said, trying for a friendly smile. "We should add you to the guest list, however. The resort likes to keep track of who's staying on the property."

"Um, okay. I guess that will be fine."

"What's your last name, Serena?" Tj asked.

"It's Wright, like Sean's."

"And how long have you been here?"

"Not long," she answered vaguely.

Tj pretended to ponder something. "I think I remember seeing you at the Inn at Angel Mountain on Monday. In the late afternoon. You were wearing that yellow jacket." Tj nodded toward the garment.

"I have to go. If you need any other information, you can ask Sean."

She started to close the door, but Tj put her foot between the door and the jamb.

"Perhaps we should have a talk," Tj suggested.

"About what?" The poor girl looked like a scared rabbit. Tj almost abandoned her mission and went to talk to Sean instead.

"I know that you were on the third floor of the Inn at around five o'clock on Monday. A witness saw you." Tj pulled out the drawing the sheriff's sketch artist had made. "Do you want to tell me what you were doing?"

The girl didn't say anything.

"You can tell me, or you can tell the sheriff. It's totally up to you."

"Okay." The girl opened the door wider. "Come in."

Tj followed her to the dining table, where they both sat down.

"What do you want to know?"

"What you were doing on the third floor of the Inn if you were staying here," Tj began.

"Is it against the law to be on the third floor?"

"It's against inn policy for people who aren't guests to be on the floor for security reasons, but I don't suppose it's technically against the law."

"I was in the bar. Sean and I had a fight. I just needed some space. I saw one of the guests get into the elevator and followed him. I told him I forgot my key. I didn't do anything. I just needed to gather my thoughts."

"I see. Is that your final answer? Remember, a man was found dead in the room you were seen standing near, and the sheriff is very interested in speaking to anyone who was in the area."

The girl looked panicked but didn't answer. Tj was about to try another approach when Sean walked in. "Tj, Serena," he greeted them. "Is everything okay?"

"Someone saw me on the third floor of the Inn after our fight on Monday," Serena answered. "Tj was just asking me about it."

"You work for the sheriff?"

Sean and Tj had spoken briefly once or twice, but they'd never shared personal information.

"No," Tj said. "At least, not officially. I guess you could say I'm an informal consultant."

"Did Serena break any laws?"

Tj hesitated. She had a few options at this point, but after a bit of thought she decided on the truth. "Not that I know of. I guess you know that Travis Davidson was murdered."

"I'd heard."

"One of the maids remembered seeing a woman in a yellow jacket outside his room just prior to the medical examiner's estimated time of death. She gave the sheriff's office this description." Tj handed Sean the drawing. "I was walking back to the house after getting a snack in the bar and saw Serena through the window."

"Did you call the sheriff?" Sean asked.

"No, and I won't unless I think it's necessary to do so."

"Maybe we should tell her," Serena suggested.

Sean shrugged. "Yeah, okay. I don't see that it can hurt." Sean sat down at the table. "Last year at nationals, when it looked like I was gaining ground on Travis in terms of points and sponsorships, he called to tell me he had proof of my participation in certain behaviors during the event that would disqualify me from the competition."

"Certain behaviors?"

"Drinking and inappropriate sexual encounters. Initially, I ignored him because I knew I was innocent, but a few months ago, I was notified that an official investigation had been opened. I argued that any documents Travis might have provided must have been falsified. I gave them what I thought was adequate documentation to provide an alibi."

"But you needed more?" Tj guessed.

"The review board argued that although I appeared to have solid alibis for most of my time at the competition, there was some that couldn't be accounted for. To make matters worse, in addition to some photos, which had to have been altered, Travis somehow managed to come up with an eyewitness to corroborate his claim. I'm not sure how he managed it, because the witness was a fairly reputable woman, but I suspect he may have blackmailed her; that seems to be his MO."

Tj looked at Serena and smiled. "So you had Dolly follow you around while you were here for the exhibition."

Sean laughed. "You noticed her, did you?"

"*Everyone* noticed her."

"Since the nationals, I've managed to make even more progress toward the number-one spot. I could tell that Travis was getting nervous, and I didn't want a repeat of the fiasco at nationals, so I asked my cousin, who happens to be a film student, to follow me around and record my every move so there would be no question of my exemplary behavior. Serena decided to use the opportunity not only to provide me with an alibi for all of my time but to do a documentary for her film class about the life of a professional snowboarder."

"I can understand why you had Serena film you, but I have to ask why you had her dress up as Dolly Parton."

"Serena suggested using a disguise. We started with the blond wig and then realized she looked a lot like Dolly. After that, one thing led to another."

"Like the enlarged chest and overuse of makeup?"

"I love Dolly Parton." Serena giggled. "She's really beautiful and so talented. It was fun to dress like her. I may have gone a bit overboard with the makeup once I got started though."

"The book she carries, as well as several other props we've outfitted her with, has cameras with date and time stamps," Sean added. "There's no way anyone can say I can't account for all of my time while I've been here."

"We even keep a camera on at night," Serena offered. "It's focused on Sean's door after he retires for the evening."

"What about tonight?" Tj asked. "You were in the room and Sean was in the bar."

"Travis is dead," Sean reminded her. "The committee dropped the investigation. I was officially informed of that a few hours ago."

"Which brings us back around to Serena's presence outside Travis's door," Tj said. "You realize this will make you a prime suspect in his murder."

"We didn't kill him," Sean assured her. "Serena has been downloading the footage we shoot every day onto discs. One of them was missing. We thought Travis must have somehow gotten hold of it. We were afraid he was planning to tamper with it, so when he left the bar to run after that woman who slapped him, Serena changed out of her Dolly costume, which would have been way too conspicuous, and into her street clothes, which she keeps in her backpack. She took a master key from the maid's cart and let herself into Travis's room. She was looking for the disc when she heard the maid in the next room and left."

"Okay," Tj decided. "Your story seems plausible to me. I'll need to see the tapes you're referring to. If the story checks out I won't report the break-in, but keep in mind that Deputy Caine gave this sketch to me, so he'll be looking for you as well. You might want to keep a low profile until everything gets straightened out."

CHAPTER 20

Sunday, February 23

Tj groaned as she looked at the clock on the nightstand beside her bed. It was the one day of the week when she was able to sleep in, and here she was, wide awake at 5:40. Deciding to give up on her quest to return to the land of dreams, she slid out of bed and pulled on her knee-high slippers. Picking up Cuervo, she cautioned Echo to be quiet as she tiptoed down the hall.

Settling Cuervo in the laundry room with his breakfast, she let Echo out of the door for his morning romp, then turned on the coffeemaker before lighting the fires in the kitchen and living room. The view from the front of the house was priceless: a huge alpine lake framed with evergreen mountains that took on a hint of red and gold in the fall, when the few deciduous trees in the area shed their leaves in preparation for winter. Although the moon continued to shine on the glassy surface of the lake, a few snowflakes began to float through the air, reminding her that another storm was forecast to hit the area by midday.

She went out to the living room with a cup of coffee, curling up on one of the sofas framing the fireplace and pulling a quilt over her legs. She sat, sipping her coffee in the dark, watching the flames in the structure her grandfather had built by hand dancing and crackling as she listened to the stillness of the early morning. Cuervo jumped up onto the couch and curled into her lap. Prior to Crissy's coming to live with them the previous fall, he'd had little use for human contact and would growl more often than not if you tried to cuddle with him. Once the other cat moved in, however, he'd staked his claim to Tj by attaching himself to her side whenever she was home.

Echo began to snore as he continued his nap in front of the fire. He was about as mellow as a dog could be, which was a good thing, because they lived in an environment where hundreds of ever-changing guests wanted to pet and play with a large black dog that looked like a small bear.

Tj leaned her head against the back of the sofa as she thought about the day ahead. The events in town started later on Sunday, giving folks who were inclined to do so a chance to attend church services before the planned competitions. When Tj's Grandma Maggie had been alive, they'd attended services every Sunday, but after she'd passed, her dad and grandpa rarely bothered to make the trip into town.

"You're up early," Ben commented as he walked into the room.

"It figures I'd wake up early on the one day I could have slept in."

"Something on your mind?"

Tj yawned. "I don't know. I guess I've just had a busy week and my brain is trying to process everything. I can't believe I'm saying this, but I think I'm actually looking forward to the carnival being over so we can settle back into a less hectic routine."

"Yeah, I have to agree. Quite a few of the guests are checking out today, and the rest will be gone by tomorrow. Things should slow down a bit until the spring-break rush. I heard they let Chelsea go," Ben offered.

"Albert Pitman provided her an alibi, in a roundabout sort of way."

"Too bad his prank landed *him* in the slammer."

"Drugging Travis was a dumb idea, but I get it. The guy had a way of pushing buttons. When I decided to look into this whole thing, Jenna, Kyle, and I made a list of suspects. I couldn't believe how long it was."

"Any luck narrowing it down?"

"Actually, we've managed to clear everyone except for Barney Johnson, Pete Quinn, Mayor Wallaby, and Corbin and Wendy Wells. Johnson claims to have been at home, but he was alone and short on proof, Pete claims to have been in Sacramento bike riding but has no receipts or other proof to back that up, Mayor Wallaby was with an individual he refuses to name, and Corbin and Wendy Wells are new suspects I haven't had a chance to talk to yet."

"Seems like now that Chelsea has been cleared and Josh has been located, you can leave it to the professionals to finish up," Ben suggested.

Tj thought about that. It was true that the only reason she'd gotten involved in the first place was to help clear Chelsea. "I guess you're right, although Dylan added Hunter to the list."

"Hunter?"

"Apparently he was at Angel Mountain on the day of Travis's murder. They argued, and then Hunter went for a drive. He didn't get home until after nine and he has no proof of his whereabouts."

"I'm sure it will get cleared up," Ben assured her. "If you

want my opinion, you should let Dylan do his thing so you can enjoy the last day of the carnival."

"It would be nice to focus on having fun. Besides, I'm not really worried. There's no way Hunter killed Travis, and I'm pretty sure Dylan doesn't really think he did either."

"I was thinking of making an egg and cheese pie for breakfast. Would you rather have bacon or sausage?"

"Either is fine. I noticed that someone bought a bunch of fruit. How about I make a big fruit salad to go with that pie?"

After sharing a leisurely breakfast with her family, Tj decided to check with the lodging staff before heading into town. Sundays tended to be busy, and with everything that was going on, that day was likely to be busier than usual. They'd had a rash of staff members calling in sick in the past few weeks, and Tj wanted to be sure they were covered.

"Morning, Tj," Serena said as Tj passed through the lodge on her way to check in with the manager on duty. "I wanted to thank you again for not ratting me out."

"Are you going home?"

"Yeah. Sean and I thought it was best, given the circumstances. He and his coach are going to stay until tomorrow, as planned."

"I'm sorry Sean had to deal with Travis and his attempt to discredit him, but it was fun watching you follow him around all week. You created quite the mystery."

Serena laughed. "It *was* fun, but I wish my charade could have been under different circumstances. It was pretty stressful for a while. Sean said he wasn't the first competitor Travis pulled that on. The other guy missed out on a major competition that cost him a key sponsor. The whole thing was such a nightmare that the guy ended up quitting snowboarding. Sean said it was a real shame because he was a really good boarder, the best he'd seen in years. I guess Travis knew he'd need to get the guy out of the way if he wanted to make it to the number-one spot."

"You should come back when you can relax and enjoy the area." Tj handed her a card. "Call me and I'll comp your room."

"Really?" Serena smiled. "That would be nice."

It seemed like the entire town had shown up for the final day of the carnival. It was an exceptional winter day: sunny, with temperatures in the low fifties. The sky was a deep blue with nary a cloud in sight. Tj was dressed casually in denim jeans, a royal blue t-shirt, and a Serenity High sweatshirt. She stood with her extended family as she waited for the snowball decathlon to start. There were five events, but each was brief, so Tj didn't expect the entire competition to take more than a couple of hours. She hoped to have plenty of time to partake in the culinary delights offered by the various vendors before the finalists in the ice princess competition took the stage a final time for the announcement of the winner.

"Is Bren nervous?" Tj asked Jenna, who was trying to work a piece of bubble gum out of Kari's hair.

"Not really. She mostly just entered to please Mom. I don't think she cares whether she wins."

"Of course she cares," Tj countered.

Jenna clipped the last few hairs, then stood back in victory. "Yeah, I guess." She began braiding Kari's long blond hair in an attempt to avoid another near disaster. "She says she doesn't, but I guess everyone wants to win on some level. How about you? Are you nervous?"

"Heck no." Tj grinned. "Why should I be nervous? This is one contest that's all but wrapped up."

"But you haven't even started," Jenna pointed out.

"Don't need to." Tj began stretching. "All I need to win is the certainty that I'm going to."

"Hey, beautiful." Hunter walked up behind Tj and kissed her on the cheek.

"Hey yourself. How's one of Paradise Lake's most wanted?" she teased.

"Not wanted." Hunter smiled. "I remembered that the hospital called when I was up near Quincy. Dylan pulled the phone records, which proved I was in that area when I received the call, giving me the alibi I needed."

"I'm glad. I was certain you didn't do it, and I was pretty sure Dylan believed that too, but with the way this crazy investigation has been going..."

"So you're still investigating?"

Tj grinned. "Not anymore."

"Glad to hear it. Since you seem to be free, want to grab some lunch after you wrap this up?"

"I promised the girls corn dogs."

"I like corn dogs."

"I promised Jenna I'd take all four girls so she could have a quiet lunch with Dennis," Tj warned. "When you get four little girls between the ages of four and eight together, it can get kind of crazy."

"I live for crazy."

"Okay, it's a date."

"Did you see the look on Connor Harrington's face when I beat his distance in the shot put by a good three feet?" Tj laughed.

"Yeah, it was pretty funny." Hunter drizzled mustard over the exterior of his hot dog on a stick. "I guess he expected you to throw like a girl."

"I don't know why he would. He should know by now that I don't do anything like a girl."

"Oh, there's a thing or two you do just like a girl."

Tj kicked Hunter under the table. The gleam in his eye was unmistakable. She suspected she knew what he was referring to, and that particular conversation was not one she wanted to have in front of her sisters.

"When do you get your trophy?" Ashley asked.

"They have a ceremony at the end of the day. Do you want some more fries?"

"I do." Kristi grabbed a handful and proceeded to stack them in such a way as to fashion a fort.

"Here, let me help you with that," Hunter offered as Kari tried to drizzle mustard on her own hot dog.

"Can we go sledding?" Gracie wondered.

"Maybe after we finish eating," Tj answered.

"Can Dr. Hunter come with us?" Gracie asked.

"Sure, if he wants to. How about it, Dr. Hunter? Do you want to try your hand at downhill propulsion via a small plastic object?"

"Sounds like fun. I haven't had the chance to partake in that particular type of transportation for quite a while."

"You might want to practice on the small hill so you don't break your coccyx," Tj teased.

"You're worried about me? I seem to remember a redheaded spitfire who bruised her callipygian backside on more than one occasion," Hunter shot back.

Tj laughed.

"How come you're talking funny?" Kari asked.

"We're just being silly," Hunter answered. "Which is something else I haven't done in quite a long time."

"I can be silly." Gracie stuck out her tongue and crossed her eyes.

"Me too." Kari giggled as she made her own funny face.

It was nice to spend time with Hunter in a relaxed atmosphere in which past and present desires weren't clouding the friendship she very much wanted to have with him. They'd never really stopped caring about each other or considering each other friends, but it had only been in the past few years that they could put raging hormones behind them and enjoy the easy camaraderie they'd always had.

"Your pants are quacking like a duck." Ashley giggled.

"Sorry, it's my phone." Hunter pulled his cell out of his pocket and checked his texts.

"Your text tone is a duck?" Tj asked. "Doesn't seem very doctor-ish."

"I like it," Hunter defended himself. "Unfortunately, I have to go. Can I get a rain check on the sledding?"

CHAPTER 21

"Mayor Wallaby has been on his phone for over half an hour," Tj informed Jenna, who had joined her and the girls at the sledding hill after her lunch with Dennis.

"So?" Jenna looked toward the parking area, where the mayor was pacing back and forth.

"Look at his face," Tj instructed. "He looks like all the steam he's building up is going to blow his toupee clear off his head any minute."

"You think he wears a toupee?"

"Either that or he needs a different barber, but that's not the point. I wonder who's making him so hot under the collar."

"Mayor Wallaby is a passionate man," Jenna reminded her. "It doesn't take much to get him worked up. Why do you care?"

"I don't." Tj sighed.

"But..." Jenna prompted.

"But I can't help finding motives for Travis's murder everywhere I look, and a passionate discussion lasting over half an hour in the middle of the winter carnival seems suspect."

"I thought you said you were going to drop your investigation and let the sheriff's office handle things," Jenna reminded her.

"I did." Tj frowned as Mayor Wallaby threw his free hand

up in the air in a gesture of pure rage. "And I am, at least in theory. It's just hard to change gears at this point."

"You could worm your way over there and see if you can hear what he's saying," Jenna suggested.

Tj hesitated. "Will you keep an eye on the girls?"

"Yeah, but don't be obvious."

"I know how to spy on someone," Tj reminded her.

Tj worked her way through the cover of the trees until she was in line with the man who was running his fingers through whatever it was that topped his head. The phone was to his ear, but he wasn't speaking. Tj assumed he was listening to whoever was on the other end of the line. Just then, he leaned against the vehicle behind him and dropped his head in defeat.

"Okay," she heard him say. "Just tell me when and where." The mayor looked at his watch. "An hour will be fine."

Then Wallaby hung up his phone and headed toward the snack shack that had been set up at the bottom of the hill. Tj watched as he ordered a beer and drained the cup in one long swig. She didn't know why she cared where the man was going, but she found that she did. Pulling her cell out of her pocket, she called Jenna, who was just on the other side of the sledding hill.

"Why are you calling me?" Jenna asked. "I can see you across the parking lot."

"Mayor Wallaby is meeting someone in an hour," she told her. "I want to follow him. Can you keep an eye on the girls until I get back?"

"The last thing you need to be doing is sneaking around after a man who looks like he's ready to kill someone," Jenna counseled her.

"I'm not going to engage him. I just want to see where he's going."

"Why don't you just call Dylan?"

"Because if he's heading out for a haircut or some other mundane chore, I'll have wasted Dylan's time and I'll look like a fool while doing it."

"What if it's dangerous?"

"Like I said, I won't engage the man. I'll follow him to see where he goes, and if it seems dangerous, I'll call Dylan."

"Okay," Jenna reluctantly agreed. "But if you get yourself killed, I'll never speak to you again."

Tj followed Mayor Wallaby through town toward the Angel Mountain ski area. She had been hoping she could watch him from the safety of her car, but when he parked in the lower lot and took the shuttle up the hill, she knew she'd have to follow him another way. Deciding to risk a parking ticket, she followed the shuttle with her vehicle and then double-parked in the red zone when she reached the village. Sliding out of her car, she tried to blend into the crowd as she followed the mayor past the shops and dining establishments, toward the gondola that transported skiers to the top of the hill. She knew there was no way she was going to be able to follow the man up the mountain, so she was relieved when he turned toward the maintenance station near the base of the lift.

"Did you bring it?" Pete Quinn stepped out from behind the heavy machinery that was housed in the garage.

Mayor Wallaby didn't say anything as he handed Pete an envelope.

Pete opened it and looked inside. "It's been nice doing business with you." He slipped the envelope into his pocket and walked back the way he'd come.

Tj assumed there must be a back door to the building. The mayor hung his head as he made his way back toward his car.

She had no idea what had just occurred, but she was fairly certain that the less-than-friendly transaction wasn't entirely legal. Tj hurried down the hill and parked her car near where the mayor had left his. She waited until the shuttle arrived and then pretended she had just arrived.

"Afternoon, Mayor," Tj greeted him as she climbed out of her vehicle. "What are you doing here?"

"Had some business. And you?"

"Same."

"Congratulations on your victory this morning."

"Will you be at the awards ceremony?" Tj asked.

"I'm heading back to the carnival now."

"You didn't happen to run into Pete Quinn while you were in the village, did you?"

The mayor paled. "No," he stammered. "Why do you ask?"

"I was supposed to meet him a while ago. I called his shop to say that I'd be late, but his staff said he wasn't there. I tried his cell, but he didn't answer. I was hoping you'd seen him so I'd know where to look."

"I hope you don't mind my saying so, but a nice girl like you shouldn't be meeting a snake like Quinn," Mayor Wallaby warned.

"Really? Why not?"

"I know he seems like a nice guy, but take my word for it when I tell you he's involved in some shady dealings. I really like you and wouldn't want to see you get hurt."

"You think he'd hurt me?" Tj was surprised Wallaby would say as much.

"I think it's best that you head back into town. You wouldn't want to be late for the awards show."

"Yeah, I guess you're right." Tj climbed back into her car. "I'll see you there."

*   *   *

Tj followed Mayor Wallaby down the mountain and back to the carnival. When she arrived, she located Jenna and the girls, and then called Dylan. She didn't know what was going on between the mayor and Pete Quinn, but she'd bet a month's pay it wasn't on the up-and-up.

"And after that?" Dylan asked when she'd filled him in on her spy mission.

"I returned to the carnival and called you," Tj answered. "I don't know what was in the envelope or what business the two men may have, but it seemed uncharacteristic for Wallaby to warn me off like that. The only thing I can think of is that the men are somehow involved in Travis's death. I thought we should check it out. Maybe talk to Quinn."

"Okay, *I'll* check it out. You stay put and wait for my call."

"But..."

"But nothing," Dylan insisted. "You've been a great help, but it's time for you to let me do my job. If Quinn is involved in Travis's death, he could be dangerous."

"But..." Tj tried again.

"Do I need to lock you up?"

"You wouldn't," Tj spat.

"I would if it was the only way to get you to do what I say. I don't want you getting hurt."

"I knew I shouldn't have let Jenna talk me into calling you."

"Tj..." Dylan warned.

"Oh, okay. I'll hang out here at the carnival, but you have to promise to call me the minute you find out what's going on."

"I promise."

*   *   *

"Talk about a male chauvinist attitude," Tj complained as she waited in line with Jenna and the girls at the ice castle.

"He's just trying to make sure you don't get hurt," Jenna reminded her.

"I'm the one who uncovered the plot," Tj insisted.

"There's a plot?"

"It seemed like a plot. Besides, I can take care of myself. I don't need some *man* protecting me."

"He's not just a man, he's a cop," Jenna pointed out. "And not only is he a cop, he's a cop who cares about you and doesn't want to see you dead."

"Yeah, I guess." Tj sighed. "It's just so frustrating to do all the hunting but then not be in on the kill."

"You've been watching too many police shows." Jenna laughed.

"How come this line is so long?" Gracie whined.

"We're almost there," Tj promised. "Are you getting tired?"

"My feet hurt."

Tj picked Gracie up. Her little sister put her arms around Tj's neck and her head on her shoulder.

"I should have reminded him how well I took care of myself when I took down Zachary's killer," Tj continued without missing a beat.

"Small ears," Jenna reminded her.

Tj looked at Ashley, who was talking to Kristi and Kari.

"He was acting like I was some helpless girl," Tj continued. "I have moves. Major moves. I could drop the guy to the ground before he knew what hit him."

"Sweetie," Jenna said, putting her arm around her best friend, "you know I love you, but you're like a dog with a bone when you get something in your head. Let it go. It's a beautiful winter day and you're at a festive event with the people you love most. Let Dylan do his job so you can do yours."

"Mine?"

"M-O-M," Jenna spelled.

"Oh, yeah. That job."

Tj rubbed her cheek against Gracie's soft curls. The poor little thing had fallen asleep. Tj would have to wake her when they got to the front of the line. She'd have a fit if she missed the castle. But for this moment Tj let herself enjoy the feel of the child in her arms. Ashley was well beyond the age at which she wanted to be held, and Tj suspected Gracie wasn't all that far behind. Tj had never thought much about having children of her own, but now that she had her sisters, it made her think how awesome it would be to have a baby in some very distant point in the future.

"You look so content," Jenna spoke. "What are you thinking about?"

"Babies," Tj answered.

Jenna laughed. "That's one of the things I love most about you. One minute you're talking assault tactics and the next you're talking babies. You're so diverse."

CHAPTER 22

As per tradition, the trophies for all of the carnival events were presented at the ceremony that took place after the final competition. And following the presentation of the trophies, the ice princess's court was introduced and the princess herself announced. Tj stood with her entire extended family as she waited for her name to be called.

"Congratulations, Coach." Connor slapped Tj on the back. "It hurt my pride a little that I was slaughtered by a girl, but I guess I should have remembered why they call you coach."

"Thanks, Connor. Second place is pretty good."

"Did you hear that Beaver Creek fell into third place behind us and Aspen Shore?"

"No, I hadn't. That means we'll face Aspen Shore next weekend at the meet in Mammoth."

"Looks like. Figured you'd want to know."

"I do. Thanks for staying on top of things. I knew I made a good choice when I appointed you captain of the team."

"Was that Connor?" Kyle asked as he walked up behind Tj just as Connor was walking away.

"Yeah."

"Was he crying the blues that you slaughtered him in three of the five events?"

"A bit. He's a good kid." Tj beamed like a proud parent. "I'm sure he'll spend the next year practicing, then come back and hand me my hat next year."

"You think he'll be back for the carnival?"

Tj shrugged. "I don't see why not. His parents live here, so I'm betting he'll be back to visit. I guess it depends on what college he decides to go to. One of his choices is Stanford. It's close enough for him to make the trip."

"It looks like you're next." Kyle nudged her toward the front of the crowd.

"And this year's snowball decathlon champion is none other than our own Tj Jensen," the mayor announced.

The crowd whistled and hollered as Tj accepted her trophy. She had always been competitive and had earned many trophies in her life, but each and every time she raised her hands to the crowd in victory she felt like Rocky Balboa at the end of his memorable fight.

"You're such a ham," Kyle teased as Tj returned to the crowd.

"I am."

"Your phone buzzed while you were parading around on the stage."

Tj took it from Kyle. There was a message from Dylan. "I'm going to go put this trophy in my car and call Dylan back," she informed Kyle. "I'll only be a minute."

"I'll be waiting. Hurry, though. You don't want to miss Bren's crowning."

Tj trotted across the high-school football field toward the parking lot. The field was covered with snow, but it was so packed down after being trampled on all weekend that it was almost like walking on cement. Dylan's message said he'd talked to Pete but had yet to corral Wallaby. That made sense; Wallaby had been busy giving out trophies. She put her trophy in her trunk and then leaned against the hood to call Dylan's cell number.

"So?" she asked as soon as he answered.

"Pete claims Wallaby owed him money and was simply repaying him. I'm pretty sure he was lying."

"Do you think the money was some sort of payoff?"

"I think that makes more sense than a simple loan payment, but Pete isn't talking. He hasn't actually broken any laws, so I can't hold him. I'm hoping Mayor Wallaby will be more forthcoming. Is he finished with the award ceremony yet?"

"Almost. He just needs to crown the ice princess."

"I think I'll head over. I can grab him as soon as he's finished."

"The gang and I are on the left side of the bandstand, about halfway back. I'll look for you."

"Okay, see you soon."

Tj hung up the phone and started back toward the crowd when she heard her name called from behind her.

"Coach Long." She smiled at Sean's coach as he walked toward her from across the parking lot. "Are you here for the crowning of the ice princess?"

"Actually, I was looking for you."

"Looks like you found me. What can I do for you?" Tj asked.

"This is kind of personal. Can we walk a bit?"

Tj hesitated. She barely knew the man. What could he possibly want to talk to her about that would be considered personal?

"I really need to get back. The family is waiting for me, and I wouldn't want to miss the crowning. Can we talk while we head in that direction?"

"Sure, no problem. I heard you got Chelsea Hanson cleared."

"I'm not sure it was my effort that ended up clearing her, but yeah, they let her go."

"Glad to hear it. She knows my daughter Pamela. They met at the X Games last winter. She seemed like a nice girl."

Tj was surprised to hear that Coach Long knew Chelsea.

"I know you're investigating Travis's murder," Roger Long continued. "I was wondering if you'd identified the killer."

Tj frowned. It seemed odd that Coach Long would ask her about her investigation. "No, not yet. Why do you ask?"

He shrugged. "Just interested. I usually try to stay on top of anything going on in the snowboard community. Travis's death was big news. Not only did it shift Sean into the number-one rank but it affected the ranking of other athletes as well."

"Yeah, I guess."

Coach Long stopped walking. He looked at Tj but didn't say anything. He had a strange look on his face that made Tj feel instantly uncomfortable.

"I really need to get back." Tj took a step back. Something wasn't right. She looked around the deserted parking lot. Everyone had already gone over to the bandstand for the crowning of the princess. "It was nice chatting with you."

"I'll walk with you," Coach Long replied. "I guess I wouldn't mind watching the crowning. I understand you had a conversation with Serena."

Is that what this whole thing was about? "I know Serena was following Sean to help document his activities because Travis was trying to frame him," Tj began. "I know Sean was driven to take such extreme action because Travis had ruined the career of another snowboarder, who I just realized must have been your athlete, Walter Tovar. I know Serena broke into Travis's room to look for a missing tape, and I understand why she did it."

"Travis was trying to frame Sean the way he framed Walter." Long was beginning to sweat, which seemed odd to Tj. Coach Long surely couldn't consider the fact that she was in on their secret to be any kind of a threat.

"I couldn't let him ruin two careers," Long continued. "Walter was like a son to me. He had unlimited potential until Travis ruined it with his lies."

"I understand," Tj offered. "Don't worry. I won't tell anyone about Serena breaking into Travis's room."

"Not only did he ruin Walter's life but he ruined Pamela's as well."

Tj was beginning to suspect that Coach Long's rant had nothing to do with her replies. It was almost as if he was trying to convince himself of something. Suddenly the whole thing was falling into place, though Tj rather wished it hadn't.

"Did you kill Travis?" Tj realized the moment *after* the words left her mouth that accusing the man of murder when they were alone in a deserted parking lot wasn't the best move she'd ever made.

"I didn't intend to." Long's body began to shake. "He had a tape of Pamela. It wasn't the type of thing a father—or anyone else, for that matter—should have to see."

"He raped her?"

"No, she was willing," Roger admitted. "Pamela loved Travis. He led her to believe he loved her too, but I know now that he only seduced her to get leverage against me. He told me if I pressed the issue of Walter's innocence, he'd post the tape online. Walter told me that he'd had enough. He wanted to quit, and I let him. I should have done more."

"So when you found out about the tape Serena was missing, you realized you had to do something to stop him," Tj theorized.

"I went to his room to try to talk some sense into him. He

was passed out in his bed. I tried to find the tape, but I couldn't. I heard people in the hall and knew I was running out of time, so I took one of the pillows from the bed and held it over his face. I'd been drinking and wasn't thinking clearly. I've regretted it ever since."

Tj suddenly realized it wasn't a good sign that Coach Long was telling her all of this.

"I understand why you might have done what you did. I probably would have done the same thing," Tj assured him. "I promise I won't tell anyone, but I really need to get back. My family is waiting for me."

"Not so fast." Roger reached his hand into his pocket.

"Is that a gun?" Tj gasped.

"'Fraid so. I was hoping to avoid this, but you insisted on snooping into matters that didn't concern you. How about we change direction so we can find somewhere a bit more private to finish our conversation?" Long pointed toward the forest, where dense trees provided the isolation she couldn't let him have. The sun had set and the sky was beginning to darken. In another twenty minutes, twilight would turn to the inky darkness of night.

"I'm not going anywhere." Tj stared Long in the eye, despite the fact that her heart was pounding and her legs were shaking.

"You realize this gun is loaded and pointing toward your chest?"

"Wouldn't be the first time." Tj sounded braver than she felt.

Coach Long began to fidget. He obviously hadn't expected her to resist. Tj knew he didn't want to shoot her out here in the open, but the minute she was camouflaged by the cover of the trees...

"Killing me won't make it better," Tj reminded him.

"What do I have to lose?" He raised the gun and took aim. He was trying to appear confident, although he was holding the gun in such a way as to suggest he was scared to death.

"You didn't have to do this," Tj stalled. "I had no idea you were involved. You could have gone home, and I'd have been none the wiser. Why did you come here to seek me out?"

"I saw you at Angel Mountain today," Coach Long explained. "I had to find out what Pete told you."

"Pete knows you killed Travis?"

"He did. He tried to blackmail me. He's dead now."

"You *killed* him?"

"On my way to find you." Coach Long let the gun slip just a little.

"I know Pete talked to Deputy Caine earlier," Tj lied. "If Pete knew you killed Travis, I'm betting he told him. Once Deputy Caine finds out Pete is dead too, you won't have much of a chance of convincing him that Pete lied. Let's face it: Your only hope is to turn yourself in. I'm sure the sheriff will go easy on you once you explain *why* you had to kill Travis."

"How do you know Pete talked?"

"I spoke to Deputy Caine earlier, and he told me he had to go because Pete was on the other line. Why else would he have called the sheriff's office unless he was going to spill the beans about what he knew?" Tj tried knew her reasoning made absolutely no sense, but she'd gotten Long's attention. "Although I guess we can ask Deputy Caine when he gets here. He's on his way to meet me. In fact, here he is now." Tj waved to someone behind him.

Coach Long turned around. Tj kicked the gun out of his hand, then rolled toward it. Then she picked it up and aimed it at him. Taking her phone out of her pocket with her free hand, she hit redial, which conveniently connected her to the man she'd pretended was already there. She really would need to thank her dad for the years of martial arts training he'd paid for. It was coming in handy more often than she liked.

"I'm in need of a big strong cop to rescue me," she said when Dylan picked up. "Do you know where I might be able to find one?"

CHAPTER 23

Thursday, February 27

"This is really nice." Tj leaned her head against Dylan's shoulder. He'd commandeered two of the resorts horses and arranged for a romantic sleigh ride for just the two of them. It was a beautiful night, with a full moon making the late-night trip through the forest easy to navigate. Dylan had brought a warm blanket for them to cuddle under, as well as a thermos of hot spiced wine to set the mood. Tj hoped that perhaps his thoughts were turning toward romance.

"With all the overtime I've been putting in during the Travis Davidson murder investigation, we really haven't had much time alone together. I wanted to see you before I left."

"Left?" Tj sat upright. So much for romance. "You're leaving?"

"Tomorrow. I have some vacation time coming, plus some comp time in lieu of overtime pay. Boggs agreed to give me ten days off. I'm going to Chicago. One way or another, I'm going to work things out with my sister. Justin needs me in his life. And I need him."

Tj's heart sank. "Are you thinking of moving back to Chicago?"

Dylan paused. "I don't know. Maybe. What I really hope is to convince Allie to move to Serenity." Dylan stopped the sleigh and turned to look at Tj. "You know I care about you, but..."

"I know," Tj finished. She'd make the same choice, if she had to, between Dylan and her sisters.

"So did you ever find out what the meeting between Pete Quinn and Mayor Wallaby was all about?" Tj changed the subject. If she didn't, she'd start to cry, and the last thing she wanted to do was make Dylan feel bad for doing what she knew he had to do.

"I talked to Wallaby." Dylan faced forward and put the horses in motion again. "He wouldn't supply details, but I gathered that Pete was blackmailing him."

"Wow, it seems Pete was a busy little blackmailer. He was getting money from Travis, Wallaby, and Roger Long. No wonder he was able to expand his store."

"Albert Pitman was likewise involved in whatever was going on, but no one is supplying details," Dylan informed her. "I guess at this point it doesn't matter. Albert is in jail, Pete is dead, and the mayor is talking about leaving the area once his term is up."

"Really?" That was news to Tj.

"He said he's being pressured by the town council to resign. They have someone else in mind for the position, but he didn't know who."

Tj smiled. "I think that's for the best. The general sentiment in town is that Wallaby has served his time and needs to move on. I guess the only other unanswered piece of the puzzle is what happened to Wendy."

"Travis had been hassling her, so she took off to visit a

friend. She claims she told her brother, but apparently he had been drinking at the time and forgot the conversation."

"Seems like that happens with him a lot."

"Yeah, Wendy says he has a problem."

Tj pulled the blanket up over her shoulders and laid her head on Dylan's shoulder again. It occurred to her that she and Dylan really had very little to talk about unless there was an active case or they'd been to a movie and could discuss it, or there were other people around to act as buffers. They'd become friends, but it was obvious to Tj that Dylan had held a large part of himself back. Not that she blamed him. His life had been so chaotic and traumatic the past year that it was only natural for him not to want to get too close to anyone new. Especially if he was going to be leaving soon. Tj realized she was on the verge of tears again.

"I heard Roy and Chelsea are dating," Tj said to break the silence.

"I guess they forged a bond when Chelsea was in jail. Roy told me he's had a thing for Chelsea for years but has always been too afraid to ask her out."

"I can see that. Chelsea has an aura about her that screams wealth and sophistication. I'm actually surprised she agreed to go out with Roy."

"Once Roy had her undivided attention, he poured on the charm. I doubt she's had better customer service at the five-star hotels she's frequented."

"I think they'll be good together. I've always liked Roy, and Chelsea seems to be mellowing as she matures."

"Matures?" Dylan laughed. "What is she, like twenty-four?"

"Chelsea has always been the entitled, spoiled, arrogant, popular girl. After Travis dumped her, she seems to have mellowed. She's...I don't know, more down to earth now, easier to approach. Trust me, the Chelsea of old would never have gone out with Roy. Of course, the Chelsea of old would never have sacrificed herself to help out Sarah either. Like I said, she's matured."

"So you didn't get along with her when you dated Hunter?"

"Not at all. Hunter and I were together for four years. Everyone—including us, at the time—assumed we'd end up married. Chelsea didn't think I was good enough for her brother and went out of her way to make sure I knew it."

"So why did the two of you break up, if you don't mind my asking?"

"Hunter's mother had his life mapped out for him before he was born. She planned for him to become a doctor, go into politics, and eventually become a state senator. After we graduated high school, she made it clear to me that it was time for Hunter to move on, and she wasn't going to let me stand in the way of her plans. Originally, Hunter and I planned to go to the same college, but in the end she convinced him to go away to some fancy university I could never afford. We managed to maintain a long-distance relationship for a couple of years, but as time went by it got harder. When he came home for Christmas break during our junior year with the daughter of one of his mother's best friends on his arm, I knew it was over."

"I'm sorry. That must have been hard."

"It was much, much worse than hard," Tj admitted. "I loved him. I'd planned to have a life with him. The fact that he'd let his mom win devastated me."

"And the girl he brought home?"

Tj shrugged. "I don't know. I guess they dated for a while. I don't think Hunter was ever really into her; I think he just caved and decided to go along with his mother's plan for his life. Maybe it was easier. His mom can be *very* persuasive. She pretty much always gets what she wants. Or at least she did at the time. I'm sure her master plan included having Hunter married off to some debutante by now."

"You and Hunter seem to have come away from your relationship as friends."

"We are. Now. I hated him at first, but after college we both ended up back in Serenity, and we decided to salvage the friendship we'd always shared."

"He seems like a good guy."

"He is. How about you? Any serious relationships before you met and married your wife?"

"Not really, although if I hadn't met Anna, I might have become serious with the woman I was dating at the time. Our relationship certainly was heading in that direction, but then I met Anna and knew she was the one I wanted to spend my life with."

Tj realized how incredibly sad it was that they'd only had a few years together. Dylan's short but intense love affair with his wife was testament to the fact that you shouldn't put things off.

"Are you still friends with her?" Tj asked. "The woman you dated before Anna?"

"Not really, although Allie is, so in an indirect way I've kept track of her life."

"She's still single?"

"She is."

Tj looked out across the dark snow-covered forest. It was a beautiful night, and she was participating in a romantic sleigh ride with a man she was beginning to develop feelings for. She really should be focusing on things of a romantic nature instead of murder cases and past love affairs.

She supposed it was the thought that he might leave for good that caused her to hold back. That and the fact that he clearly had other things on his mind than romance and new relationships.

"By the way, I want to thank you for what you did for Ashley. She came home from school yesterday all smiles after she was the special guest at the safety assembly. She told me that everyone was being so nice to her, including Loretta. In fact, Loretta invited her to her party."

"She didn't miss it?"

"No, it's Saturday. Loretta's birthday was Monday, but they decided not to have the party the same weekend as the winter carnival."

"So is Ashley going to go to the party?" Dylan asked.

"Surprisingly, yes. To be honest, I would have thought Ashley wouldn't want to go after everything that happened, but she told me that Deputy Dylan said that sometimes when people around us act immature, we have to be the bigger person. I guess what you told her sank in, because she's decided to be the better person and let bygones be bygones. So thank you. I doubt anything I could have said would have made as much of an impact on her."

"I'm happy I could help."

"This parenting thing is hard," Tj admitted. "I guess I get now why parents come in pairs."

Dylan got a distant look on his face. Tj realized that her innocent comment had probably returned his thoughts to Justin and his responsibility to him. Tj didn't know if she and Dylan would ever have their time together, but she hoped they would. Deep in her heart, she knew they could have had something special together if only they'd met in a different time and place, under different circumstances.

KATHI DALEY

Kathi Daley lives with her husband, kids, grandkids, and Bernese mountain dogs in beautiful Lake Tahoe. When she isn't writing, she likes to read (preferably at the beach or by the fire), cook (preferably something with chocolate or cheese), and garden (planting and planning, not weeding). She also enjoys spending time in the water, hiking, biking, and snowshoeing. Kathi uses the mountain setting in which she lives, along with the animals (wild and domestic) that share her home, as inspiration for her five cozy mystery series: Zoe Donovan, Whales and Tails Island, Tj Jensen, Sand and Sea Hawaiian, and Seacliff High Teen.

**The Tj Jensen Mystery Series
by Kathi Daley**

Henery Press Mystery Books

And finally, before you go...
Here are a few other mysteries
you might enjoy:

LOWCOUNTRY BOIL

Susan M. Boyer

A Liz Talbot Mystery (#1)

Private Investigator Liz Talbot is a modern Southern belle: she blesses hearts and takes names. She carries her Sig 9 in her Kate Spade handbag, and her golden retriever, Rhett, rides shotgun in her hybrid Escape. When her grandmother is murdered, Liz hightails it back to her South Carolina island home to find the killer.

She's fit to be tied when her police-chief brother shuts her out of the investigation, so she opens her own. Then her long-dead best friend pops in and things really get complicated. When more folks start turning up dead in this small seaside town, Liz must use more than just her wits and charm to keep her family safe, chase down clues from the hereafter, and catch a psychopath before he catches her.

Available at booksellers nationwide and online

Visit www.henerypress.com for details

PILLOW STALK

Diane Vallere

A Madison Night Mystery (#1)

Interior Decorator Madison Night might look like a throwback to the sixties, but as business owner and landlord, she proves that independent women can have it all. But when a killer targets women dressed in her signature style—estate sale vintage to play up her resemblance to fave actress Doris Day—what makes her unique might make her dead.

The local detective connects the new crime to a twenty-year old cold case, and Madison's long-trusted contractor emerges as the leading suspect. As the body count piles up, Madison uncovers a Soviet spy, a campaign to destroy all Doris Day movies, and six minutes of film that will change her life forever.

Available at booksellers nationwide and online

Visit www.henerypress.com for details

BOARD STIFF
Kendel Lynn

An Elliott Lisbon Mystery (#1)

As director of the Ballantyne Foundation on Sea Pine Island, SC, Elliott Lisbon scratches her detective itch by performing discreet inquiries for Foundation donors. Usually nothing more serious than retrieving a pilfered Pomeranian. Until Jane Hatting, Ballantyne board chair, is accused of murder. The Ballantyne's reputation tanks, Jane's headed to a jail cell, and Elliott's sexy ex is the new lieutenant in town.

Armed with moxie and her Mini Coop, Elliott uncovers a trail of blackmail schemes, gambling debts, illicit affairs, and investment scams. But the deeper she digs to clear Jane's name, the guiltier Jane looks. The closer she gets to the truth, the more treacherous her investigation becomes. With victims piling up faster than shells at a clambake, Elliott realizes she's next on the killer's list.

Available at booksellers nationwide and online

Visit www.henerypress.com for details

Made in the USA
Coppell, TX
07 February 2024